Permian
Emissary of the Extinct

Devyn Regueira

Copyright © 2019 Devyn Regueira

ISBN: 9781080392162

To my grandfather, Luis Regueira, and all the bygone participants of all the bygone eras.

INSTALLMENT ONE

"Welcome, welcome, pleasure to see you, please pick a seat and stick to it."

Twenty-nine, lanky, bespectacled, and a victim of his own first name, Every Daniels could not be blamed for pinning authoritativeness to the end of his long list of allergies. It was only in the early moments of his first lecture that he realized there might be a cure.

"Settle down, pilgrims."

If there was a cure for awkward humor, Every hadn't begun to look.

"Welcome to General Anthro studies, week two. I have no doubt that you've all had your fill of syllabus jargon, but there's a final announcement relating to the class that I have to make before we can finally get our hands dirty."

Every took a breath deep enough to know the shape of his ribcage behind the second of five flannel shirts he cycled through in accordance with a weekly ritual.

"Today marks our third meeting. For me, it will be the last."

Every could not blame his students for their lack of response. A pair of hour-and-a-half long lectures, neither having strayed far from test scheduling and the evils of plagiarism, had been poor facilitators of the bond he'd grown so fond of across his tenure. Some, no doubt those especially meticulous few who researched every professor before committing themselves to a class, chattered amongst themselves.

"I've left a box of tissues for each of you under your desks. Feel free to use them. There is no judgement here."

One student, gullible or curious or genuinely distressed - none could be sure - took too conspicuous a glance between her feet. There was no box of tissues, only laughter.

"Quiet down, everyone, please. Ma'am, I do appreciate the sentiment."

The freshman transfer from Japan hid behind her hair and slouched in her seat. Every continued despite the twinge of guilt.

"I have not been fired, in case you were wondering. Still too crafty for that. No, I am leaving of my own accord, and the accord of our Federal government, *who art in Heaven*, and for a very special reason."

Every's hands were drawn together in false prayer, and his eyes remained closed when he parted them.

"I think I told you that I was invited to spend the long weekend in Russia - Siberia, specifically. To be true, I had been given no explanation, and it would be fair to say I had no reason to expect a warmer welcome than Napoleon himself."

A smile then rooted itself across the professor's face, unique before an auditorium that brimmed with phone-lit chins and supported a thimble's worth of polite attention. Every still could not blame them for their disinterest, and certainly he did not expect it to last.

"It's not every day you get a ticket in the mail with your name on it, out of the blue, no return address to speak of. But after four weeks trying to talk myself out of it ended in a hung jury, I layered my cat's bowl with two days dry and two days wet and hopped in a cab. Even Napoleon got a private island out of his visit. What's the worst that could happen to me?"

Someone coughed in a manufactured way. Two more came in answer, and Every identified the matching fraternity hats on their heads, and still he harbored no resentment toward them. Due time.

"I was met at the airport - pardon - *at the tarmac* - by fifteen blacked-out, bulletproofed S-classes. A motorcade packed with ten Russian generals for each they thought the French army was worth and fifty times the horsepower."

Every adjusted his glasses as the coughing reached a crescendo.

"I know it sounds like I'm bragging, *I know*, but I'll ask that you reserve your judgements. I haven't had much cause to train myself in the art of humility before now."

"Were they wearing beaver hats?"

The voice was male and slurred. Beginning at 11:30 sharp, his first of two Tuesday-Thursday lectures, Every passively wondered whether it were the slur of a long night or an early start.

"Many of them were, now that I think about it."

"In Soviet Russia, radio listen to you."

Early start. Years of therapy and stringent routine had made Every's confidence robust enough to allow for public speaking, a prerequisite for his current position to be sure. Neither were enough in their own right, however, to silence a deep seated social anxiety that survived to nag him in echoes from early childhood.

"Quite right, young man. And you can be sure that the practice outlived the Union."

Every glanced at the entrance. Hung above the double doors, an analog clock scolded him for being too liberal with his time.

"Allow me to get to the point. I'll ask that you put your phones away now. Treat the next hour like a test. If I see a screen, it means cheating. Cheating means expulsion."

More coughing.

"A man in, well, a beaver hat, took my suitcase. Another man in another hat took me by the arm. After a short walk and a conversation more one-sided than racquetball, they sat me all alone in the back of a limousine. A long drive and two paper bags full of vomit later, my new friends and I squeezed into a single prop plane to begin an unguided tour of the motherland from ten thousand feet.

"Flying makes me nervous, if you can believe it, so the only sightseeing I did was of a rosary the pilot was kind enough to lend me when the turbulence hit. I regret that now."

Having rehearsed it since he stepped onto the international flight home, this was the point in the account that Every expected would begin to draw attention. Even the girl he'd played no small part in humiliating parted her bangs.

"We landed on an asphalt strip that looked like it hadn't had the chance to dry. It could've been on fire, didn't make a difference to me so long as it was close to sea level. But the second I was out of that cabin, the *moment* my feet were underneath me, I nearly knocked myself out trying to get back inside."

"What was it?" asked the Japanese student.

"Was it a pretty girl?" proposed the binge drinker.

"Worse" admitted Every. He preceded his next sentence, and nearly every sentence thereafter, with a sip from the bottle his students could be forgiven for assuming was filled with water.

"I suppose it's probably just the second semester here for most of you, but has anyone had the opportunity to take Professor Bonman's Earth History course?"

A half-dozen hands cast their fluorescent shadows across rows of cushioned seats.

"Count yourselves lucky, Bonman is one of our best," Every shook his head, "and something tells me this will be his last semester, too. You," a well groomed fingernail implicated the student with their hand held highest, "did he cover the Permian-Triassic extinction event? You may remember it as the 'Great Dying'. Bonman prefers the colloquial."

"He did. Scared the shit outta me."

Older perhaps than Every himself, the southern hemisphere of a Marine Corps tattoo peeking out beneath his sleeve, the student had intelligent eyes that gave no indication of regret for his choice in words. Every smiled. He liked these sorts of students. Especially today.

"As it should have. Would you be so kind as to share what you can remember regarding the nature of the events that led to the Great Dying?"

The man cracked his knuckles, calloused, and his neck, also tattooed.

"Volcanism, mainly. But there were a lot of reasons. A 'confluence', I think Professor B. put it."

"Sounds like him. Did Professor B. mention *where* the volcanism occurred?"

"Siberia. Or whatever the good people of Pangea would have called Siberia back then."

Every's heart raced, pumping in direct proportion to the pinpricks and sweat that spread as conquerors from end to end of him. He knew, as a matter of context, that this student had made a joke. All that Every knew as a matter of absolute fact was that it was, in any case, no longer of any consequence.

"Professor Bonman - did he have time to discuss the world before and directly after this event? In other words, what can you tell us, if anything, about the variety of life preceding and following the purported spike in volcanism?"

"Not much, he always focused more on the geology. The man loves his rocks."

"That he does. Can anyone here pick up where Bonman left off, then?"

It was extremely apparent that the Japanese student had anticipated this question, and that she'd spent some minutes in silent deliberation over whether volunteering her answer justified the attention. Her professor watched the mental conflict unfold, a conflict he knew intimately, and was in no small way impressed when her hand rose in sheepish tribute.

"You, young lady near the front."

Her accent was slight, her English impeccable.

"The Permian period, the last of the Paleozoic, culminated in the Great Dying. Megafauna had finally proliferated on land, as it had for hundreds of millions of years at sea. The most prolific were, *colloquially*, 'mammal like reptiles', also called stem or proto mammals."

Every smiled and shook his head, listening with great satisfaction as if to a session his first psychiatrist had insisted on recording.

"Nobody told me we had a paleontology major in the class, let alone a PHD."

Every disguised another glance at the clock behind his upturned water bottle. The young woman was blushing by the time he set it down.

"Please, continue. You're doing a better job of it than I can, and this is quite important."

She nodded.

"Descending from the first reptiles to evolve terrestrial egg laying and water-tight scaly hides, proto-mammals were not constrained by proximity to bodies of water like amphibians continue to be. They are also considered to be our own ancestors, at least those that filled ecological niches well suited to endure a mass extinction event."

"Such as?"

"Such as burrowing for shelter."

"And?"

Her eyebrows slanted harshly downward, as if there were some physical demand in thinking as hard as she now had the occasion to.

"And omnivorousness. General adaptability."

"Ding ding ding. So, young lady," another sip, "you contend that our ancestors developed this adaptivity *prior* to the extinction event, a stroke of luck that insulated them from those circumstances which claimed their larger and more specialized cousins, rather than *following* it in some Hail Mary response to those same circumstances. Is that correct?"

"Yes."

"And how do you know this? How do *we* know this?"

"The fossil record, sir."

"DING DING DING!"

Every slammed his fast-depleting water bottle on the desk with enthusiasm enough to generate an auditorium wide debate regarding its contents.

"Meet my new favorite student, everyone! I would ask your name, ma'am, but by now it might just hurt too much. Please, while we all have this time together - *please* give us your best estimate of the percentage of individual animals that fossilize."

"Small, tiny. A fraction of a fraction of a percent."

"And of that fraction, what percentage can our own species proclaim to have unearthed?"

"That percentage is statistically negligible."

"*Statistically negligible.* That, my friend, is poetry."

Every's bottle was empty.

"So, of that negligible number plucked from a modicum of possibility, is it feasible that we've identified, categorized, and Latinized the names of every critter who scuttled along the eons on four legs or two?"

"We almost certainly never will."

"I love an optimist."

The professor parted two tidy stacks of manilla folders to create a throne for himself on the desk. His legs dangling, Every produced a second water bottle that he promptly unscrewed with his back teeth.

"You touched on the evolution of hard-shelled eggs. We can thank the fossil record for our understanding of that critical development too, can't we?"

"Yes, professor, we -"

"Call me Every. Every - ha - *every*-one else does."

"Yes, Every, eggs can fossilize as well under the correct circumstances. We know by their deaths in proximity to near-viable embryos, for example, that some dinosaurs evolved rudimentary maternal care behavior tantamount to those of extant bird species."

"Woah! Let's not get ahead of ourselves, favorite student. Why jump to the mesozoic when we have a deposit of tenderly nurtured eggs dating back to our favorite alliterative epoch to ponder? A deposit the size of *Rhode Island*, no less."

Every's favorite student looked confused and uncomfortable, the orchestra of coughs and fraternal chit-chat doing nothing to assuage either.

"I suppose I'm being unfair. Allow me to explain."

First would come another sip, a long look at the clock, and a wobbling survey of his audience meant to ensure that his rules regarding phones continued to be minded.

"We left off in Siberia, *a rosary in a heathen's hand*, and a surprise. That surprise was a hole - NO - it was two holes just beyond the end of the landing strip, three hundred feet deep a piece, divided by a wall of earth no broader than yours' truly at the shoulders - like the Venn diagram that never was."

Giggling.

"They were more like canyons than holes, really. But the big-wig Federal agent who explained them to me said hole, so we'll stick to it. 'Each hole is about half the size of Rhode Island,' he says. He was an American, the first I'd seen and a surprise all its own. It was only natural that the American fellow would choose a state for his size comparison, albeit the littlest one, but a mighty state nonetheless."

Unadulterated laughter reigned in the auditorium. None of the students, in their delight, felt compelled toward subtlety while the professor himself brandished his blood alcohol content with impunity.

"So we're standing at the precipice of this city-sized-state-sized chasm, me and the American, and I am in awe. So I say - so I say 'sir, what is this place? I'd have seen such a place on Google Earth, I know it!' And the man tells me, verbatim, 'Google Earth is clip art beside what we've got.' Fair enough, I tell him, but you haven't explained the holes."

"So, class, does anyone want to take a shot," Every took a shot, "at what his answer was?"

A new voice staked its claim.

"Impact craters?"

"Wrong."

"Calderas?"

"Creative! No. Try again."

More like a college mascot than an internationally celebrated professor, Every was, by now, pacing before his class, flapping his arms to churn their interest, and demonstrating his own by cupping a hand behind his ear to filter answers from the general buzz.

Then came a familiar voice, small and timid and more heavily accented amidst all the excitement. It was an answer more like a stroke of genius than of luck, a contention made by a person born to solve puzzles without pictures on the box. Every liked to think he'd have given that sort of answer.

"A nest?"

Every dropped to both knees across from her.

"Tell me your name, young lady."

"I am called Airi."

"Airi," Every thrust himself to his feet, "you are correct. You are - well, you are half correct. But half correct is good enough. Everyone!"

Every clapped his hands, at once startling Airi and instigating a chant of her name with a cluster of Greek lettered clothing for its epicenter. Every spoke the name as well, above all the others until they held their tongues, and then again much more softly.

"Airi... You are correct. One of the holes, spanning one-hundred-and fifty-vertical feet for half of Rhode Island's perimeter, is *lined* in *rows* of fossilized eggs. *Rows*. Before we discuss how spectacular that is, why don't you tell me how you figured it out?"

"Context, sir."

"Your modesty is enchanting. You haven't ceased to amaze me, Yairi, so please don't start now. Because, because - now I must ask whether you have enough context left in the tank to explain the purpose of the second hole."

Airi spent the next few seconds in a problem-solver's reverie. She spoke again sooner than Every could have expected, and although her answer arrived in the form of another question, her professor reacted as though it were the correct one.

"What do you mean *purpose?*"

"You are special, aren't you? Pay attention, class, genius seldom strikes twice in the same place. I can see it on Annie here's face. She has another question on her mind. Please, Annie, ask away."

"How could any species apart from our own have moved such volumes of earth?"

Designed to encourage her to continue her train of thought, Every made a gesture more like that of a rude customer in the periphery of his overwhelmed waitress.

"No terrestrial vertebrate could possibly lay so many eggs in its lifetime. There must have been... cooperation between many individuals of the same species. A communal nest, constructed to be populated in what you have described as *rows*. As if deliberately - as if *meticulously*. Is that possible, Every?"

"It is possible. I will tell you how, my dearest Aimee, when you tell me what was in the second hole."

"It was a grave, wasn't it?"

Every's head pivoted as if toward a creak in his empty house at midnight. His eyes were wide when they fell upon the marine, astonished by his answer and distraught to see him gathering his things to leave.

"I think you've had enough, professor."

Every had the bottle to his lips before the soldier could hope to snatch it, and drained before the class could process what was happening.

"You should be ashamed of yourself."

The marine made for the exit. Every made it first.

"You should be proud of yourself!"

His body planted against the double doors, his neck craned, and his eyes glued to the narrow face of an inverted clock - Every knew his time was up.

The men stood virtually chest to chest, and so when they spoke it was a conflict waged in whispers.

"A grave. A *mass* grave of *bipedal, humanoid, proto mammals*.

"Not the product of some calamity, not a Stalinist pile of undesirables, a *deliberate, meticulous, burial infrastructure* dating back before the first dinosaur evolved a pelvis fit for diapers!"

"Get out of my way."

"I will. I promise you I will."

His back to the class and the barrel of Every's gun pressed discreetly to his sternum, the marine lifted his hands in submission and began the retreat to his seat.

"Wait."

Every stuffed the weapon back into his pants before any of the countless eyes trained on their exchange could catch a glimpse of its deciding factor.

"You may sit."

No other student had cause for alarm when the marine returned to his seat, but most had cause for discomfort when the professor bolted the double doors shut.

"Don't worry about that folks, just a friendly chat. What I am about to tell you all is - is very *sensitive*. Listen closely, if you will, and I may be inclined to let you out a few minutes early."

Every's extension of good will succeeded in abating much of the tension. His deteriorating sobriety even injected some humor back into the room when he retook its center stage.

"Two of your classmates have already impressed me very much today. Upon foundations of sense and knowledge, they have helped paint a portrait of the fantastic development to which I bore personal witness. I cannot blame them, thus, for missing two final details - two *critical* questions you should all be asking yourselves, right now. So please, someone, will you speak out and join the storied ranks of these bright young minds so deserving of our praise?"

Airi did not give her classmates the chance.

"Why would they invite an anthropologist to a paleontological dig?"

Every smiled softly, sadly.

"That is the first question, and I have no doubt that some of you have already worked out the second."

Every stared without subtlety at the marine, both men sweating profusely in a room artificially chilled.

"You choose, Airi. Would you like me to answer the first question before or after you pose the second?"

"I would like to know the first answer now, Every."

"Very well.

"The day my invitation was sent, the joint U.S. - Ruski team hoped I could cast doubt on their suspicions that the construction and design of the craters were intelligent by necessity. By the time I opened my mailbox, they'd already decided my time would be better spent analyzing the apparent *writing* that lined what was once the upper lip of the nesting hole."

Gasps sounded from those students that Every may once have considered gullible, chides and giggles from those he might have called closed minded.

"And I did analyze it, briefly. Not long enough to solve a crossword puzzle, really, because - because, I didn't know it, but before I set foot on a plane - "

Filtered through a prism of vodka, Every's words remained ever slurred, but along the way had shed all tone and humor. Left behind was a husk of his former enthusiasm, only the droll, lifeless cadence of a man burdened by reality at its most solemn.

"- before I set foot on a plane, they'd already decoded the nest etchings. Not in their entirety, of course, but enough to get the gist. By then they understood that it was more math than language. A sequence, to be specific. I had a more important job now, 'the most important job', the American said. Because they'd found a second series of etchings, this one in the grave hole, inscribed into a ring of granite that had no business where it was. So I looked like I'd been asked to, repelling myself along the sheer cliff face, squinting and petrified. I looked long and hard, and at the end I had no doubt to cast and no alternative to offer."

Every left his flannel as a damp pile on the carpet before retaking his seat on the desk, the uncomfortable lump he sat upon a harrowing reminder of what awaited him.

"So now you know. Before we get to that pesky second question you've all been dancing around, I would like to extend you, soldier, the opportunity to ask me anything you like. Free reign - unabated access. You've earned my respect today, and you've certainly earned the right to some clarity."

The marine considered exploiting his moment at the dais to make his classmates aware of the impending danger presently wedged beneath their professor, but resolved in the course of moments that it would be better spent distracting the man with the gun.

"What were the etchings above the nest - the sequence? What did it describe?"

Every coughed into his hand, preparation for a statement he intended to fulfill on a single breath.

"Deoxyribonucleic acid. The index, table of contents, and bibliography of a forgotten organism. The - the *entire genome* of an extinct species of proto mammal, its constituent nucleotides denoted, respectively, by points, line segments, triangles, and squares - and in such a way that time could not produce an eraser fit for the task of cleaning the slate."

Airi's jaw rested upon her desk when the man who'd lost his mind focused its attentions upon her.

"You, Aimee, are my favorite student. And so you will be extended the same courtesy."

"I - I don't…"

"Would you like to ask about the second inscription ring?"
A nod.

"I'm glad you did. The mass grave crater, in all its morbid glory, was not inscribed with a sequence in the conventional way of thinking - not like the nest. It was a ring of pictures, rather, like baby's carousel far above an audience of the lost members of that species. I don't think it was for them, though. Not really.

"The pictures were carved into panels of homogeneous size and in increments of approximately one-point-five-eight-three centimeters. And when I say 'approximately', people, I mean to say that our measurements were approximate - not the panels. Those were implemented with what appears to be mechanical precision. Each image was a moment in time, a flash-frozen glimpse at the constellations that would be visible across the Siberian night. These were not glimpses of this species' collective moment in time, mind you - but of *all time*. Nine-and-a-half million half-inch scenes, spanning eighty-five miles and nearly ten billion years, from the presumed beginning of our solar system to the predicted end, each scene summarizing our galactic scenario at a cosmic instant of one thousand years. And it was... perfect."

Every began to shake.

"It was so perfect that it was beautiful, so beautiful that it was horrible. And never did it seem more horrible than the moment I followed their pattern, on a hunch, to the approximate date of the Great Dying."

Many students had become upset. Several stood to leave. Every did not bother attempting to persuade them to stay and listen, it seemed a much easier thing to slam his pistol on the desk.

"Sit down. You will be free to go in five minutes. If I see or hear a phone, rest assured that time will be added."

Both Every's demands were respected.

"Blank. One panel situated in the series we estimated should encompass their Great Dying was scrubbed clean, or scraped, rather, from the face of the timeline. I had analyzed hundreds of scenes by now, each as pristine as the last - devoid of so much as a scratch to tarnish their message. My hunch supported, my hypothesis taking shape, I was chauffeured back in time - many millions of years, many *many* thousands of images, to the approximate extinction between the Devonian period and the Carboniferous. Sure as - well, sure as *shit*, just where we predicted we'd find it - a panel had been tampered with."

Every pointed one finger at the ceiling while another rested on the trigger.

"It was not a total validation of my suspicions, however, only another piece of the puzzle. Because where the panel seemed to have been scrubbed by the same process as the scene corresponding to the

Permian extinction, they were distinct in the *degree* to which they had been defaced. Further investigation of the Permian etching revealed 97% destruction, the Devonian a meager 76%. Can anyone tell why those numbers sound familiar?"

Not so much as a cough. All to insulate the auditorium from complete silence was the ticking of a clock that Every kept at all times in the corner of his eye.

"I apologize, people, I think we may miss our mark for early dismissal. In any case, I will try my best to get you out of here in time for a late lunch.

"Where was I? Oh, right. The Devonian. An extinction event characterized by the devastation wrought upon oceanic biodiversity. Modern estimates place total global special loss between seventy and eighty percent."

Every's eyelids independently drooped as he swept his gaze across a captive audience.

"As for the Permian, ninety-seven percent is right on the money. This unsettling coincidence was not lost on me or my slavic colleagues, and so we, upon our all-terrain chariots, journeyed across the ages, taking pit stops at every mass or minor extinction event we could Google. Imagine our surprise when, *time after time*, our suspicions were confirmed, our excursions validated, our temporal approximations snugly placed in the margin of error and our species-loss calculations proven more or less reputable by the percentile vandalism of primordial granite.

"Imagine - *imagine*, if you will, when the - when the skinny anthropologist, the Anthro 101 professor fulfilling his commitment as emissary between the scientific field and our brightest young minds - imagine when *Every Daniels* had another hunch. Imagine what he thought, that nervous wreck, that therapy addict, that speaker in the third person - imagine how he felt when he repelled from the lip of that crater to pinpoint his own date in the sun and found it wiped clean, lost without a trace, one-hundred-percent *gone*."

Beep beep beep. Beep beep beep. Every heard the muffled voices of half a dozen 9-1-1 operators as the clock struck one o'clock. The class had called his bluff. It did not matter now.

"Imagine, Aimee, how he must have felt."

Airi saw her life flash before her eyes as if from the barrel of the gun now level with her face.

"Tell me, Aimee, *tell me*."

"He felt - "

"Tell me!"

"I'm sorry! My God - he felt scared, frightened! He was frightened!"

Every cocked the pistol.

"Yes he was. First he was frightened by what he presumed to be the abrupt certain end of his species foretold an inch from his face. What frightened him more, Aimee, was a second realization. There were no coincidences in Siberia, that much was clear to me."

Someone pressed on the doors from outside. Some students began to call for help, others began to cry. The doors shook more insistently, and so too did the voices of the students.

"Listen to me!"

Every fired. Dust and insulation rained upon the head of the girl who believed she had just overheard the commission of her own murder.

"Listen. To. Me.

"There *could be no coincidences*. Not when you are face to face with the ruins of a species that could exactly predict dozens of extinctions, with the phenomena responsible being equally varied, millions of years after their own demise. If they had learned the date of their own destruction, who is to say they did not predict the nature of the world they'd leave behind? The nature of their descendants, directly or not? What, if not pure, cruel coincidence, would compel them to supply the ingredients for their existence - the *recipe for their revival* - in a hole that necessitates intelligence to reach, in a way that demands intelligence to transcribe, within yards of a timeline that an intelligent species could only deduce predicts their own *annihilation?*"

An intermission in the shaking after Every's warning shot had been brief, and now the doors rocked with the impact of a shoulder or booted foot. Every heard sirens now. Due time.

"These questions will be yours to ponder. As I said, this will be my final lecture. You will have many more, I hope, so whatever you think of me - however you remember our time together, I would only ask that you keep an open mind regarding today's material. There will be skeptics. There always are. For now, I would ask that you listen politely while Aimee, our best and brightest student, poses that second question we've all been waiting for."

"Every…"

"Please, Aimee. We don't have long. Ask away."

Airi looked to her left. The marine had chosen a seat in the front row after his skirmish with the professor, perfectly placed to offer his classmate what solidarity he could and a nod of encouragement.

"Why would the government let you tell us all of this, Every?"

"You never cease to amaze me. They would not, Aimee. They would not."

Every pressed the muzzle of the first gun he'd ever owned to a mind he'd worked so long to control, and then his slate was clean.

INSTALLMENT TWO

Alvin Bonman grew up on an island. It was not an island in the conventional sense - not a deposit of sand anchored by mangroves, not a reef with ambitions above and beyond its fluid atmosphere. Alvin was raised on an island in the way that a man can grow in his isolation, in his stubbornness, or in his resolve to become one.

Alvin's island was a hill. West Virginian hardwood forests were his beaches, gorilla glue reinforced Sketchers and a neck-high walking stick his raft, a retired stone quarry his escape on the horizon.

Much like a commercial jet crawling across the Pacific sky - gradual enough to tease the marooned with reminders that civilization pressed onward; brisk enough to miss the declaration of survival he told in smoke behind the curve of the Earth - Alvin's mother was around, occasionally, but what benefit was it to him?

Alvin's mother often claimed to have more part-time jobs on her schedule than wardrobes in her closet. Mrs. Bonman was not known to her son as a liar, and by the urgency that cheapened those elusive moments they did spend together he came to doubt that she had any to waste on hyperbole.

As all his mother's waking hours were committed to that scramble between jobs and uniforms and banks and buses, and his father's final waking hour having come to pass in some dreary Vietnamese jungle, precious few of Alvin's summer days had been spent on a parent's hip. Those days were dedicated instead to his island, and his raft, and to his escape.

Young Alvin's daily routine began at the foot of his ill-designed gravel slope of a driveway. It ended, weather permitting, a mile-and-a-half away at the equally precarious rim of the quarry. From there he preferred to make his descent barefoot, any grip his shoes may have afforded their first or second owners functionally lost. With the grace of a billy-goat, with calloused feet for hooves, he'd slip, slide, gallop, and survive his way down sixty feet of loose rock to the shore of a stagnant runoff pool.

Not unlike a smudged face on a volleyball, Alvin, in his solitude, learned to manufacture intimacy from the inanimate. Parents and friends may have been inaccessible from his island, but there was one resource present in abundance. Alvin took a liking to rocks, and, so far as he could tell, rocks took a liking to him.

Company became curiosity, affection became infatuation, and so Alvin's geology career began, unbeknownst to him, barefoot in the quarry at the age of fourteen.

His experiments were crude at the start. Many rocks were smashed, several metric tons of rubble examined and categorized, dozens of beetles sacrificed to further his knowledge of physical properties no less fundamental than weight or density. Gradually Alvin matured, and, to the great relief of the insect population, so too did his methods.

From fourteen onward, Alvin dedicated every autumn, winter, and spring to financing his research in the quarry. By his fifteenth summer, Alvin's walking stick had been sidelined in favor of a yard sale pick-axe. His sixteenth and seventeenth excursions were benefited by several outdated geology textbooks he'd negotiated into affordability from the local college. It was only some months later that Alvin discovered that the school had intentions to shred those books that very afternoon, and still he regarded the exchange a steal, and himself the beneficiary.

By eighteen, Alvin possessed a refurbished microscope and a desk to set it on, a pile of samples eager to share their secrets, a proud mother, and a full scholarship to his choice of the country's elite universities.

At fifty-two, Alvin's microscope looked much the same as it had the day he salvaged it from a pile of Salvation Army riffraff. The desk supporting it was varnished and expensive, the walls surrounding it chaotic with degrees and accolades.

In truth, Alvin's microscope represented the sum of his childhood keepsakes; a lonely memento from a lonelier time. Even his proud mother was remembered only as a pixelated smile behind the desktop clutter of a busy professor.

That invasive thought struck for the thousandth time. Alvin shuddered.

It wasn't until he'd rearranged every file and folder on the screen that his despair had sufficiently dulled for cohesive thought. He could see his mother now; his best surviving glimpse of her. She was suspended in time as his desktop background, a younger woman but not a young one, a woman beaming with pride beside the son, then a new college graduate, who'd given her a reason.

Desperate to avoid the cyclical trap of grief and rumination he'd fallen victim to for the three months since her death, Alvin Bonman locked his screen. Her face was displaced by his own muted reflection - a middle-aged black man, electively bald since Michael Jordan's first triple-double found fashion in what had been misfortune.

Alvin's wristwatch read 09:43 and his calendar Tuesday. It was the perfect time for a late breakfast, and it was a peculiar time for a knock on his door.

"Office hours start at 11:00!"

The knocker was undeterred.

"Did you miss the memo on daylight savings time?"

Knocking became pounding. Professor Bonman's prized calaverite-specimen-turned-paperweight began to vibrate at the perfect frequency to move across his desk.

"Alright! Christ, just give me a minute."

One part meticulous nature and three parts agitation, Bonman took his time relocating the glass-encased mineral sample to the safety of his bookshelf.

"So what exactly can I help you - god dammit, Every."

The man behind the door and its bombardment was, despite appearances, not a student. Every Daniels was a friend. He was not an *old friend* - be that distinction measured in terms of years and birthdays or semesters of association - but, in Alvin's mind, he was a good friend.

"You scared half the shit right out of me, pounding on the door like that! I'd be pissed at you if my laxative bill weren't getting higher by the month."

Every was a vocal fan of Alvin's inventive vulgarity, but the young professor did not seem in the mood for humor when he sealed the office door behind him. A baker's foot shorter, Alvin had to crane his neck to notice how pale Every's face had become since last they spoke.

"Christ kid, were they feeding you snow in Russia? You're whiter than old dog shit."

Every's lips puckered and his silence remained, long enough for Alvin to flirt with the possibility that he'd teased a step too far. The uneasy silence gradually outlasted what he'd expect if that were the case, and so he gestured to the chair across from his own and resolved to get his friend talking in time for brunch.

"Something bothering you, kid?"

"Yes."

"Would it be safe to assume that that something happened in Siberia?"

"… Yes."

The crown jewel of his position as head of Geology and a source of envy among his less tenured colleagues, the window behind Alvin's desk directly overlooked UC Berkley's scenic quad. Mid-morning sun burrowed through slats in its shutters and painted rungs into the back of his neck.

"Did the Russians rough you up or something? Clamp a twelve volt to your nipples and make you sing *Be Glorious, our free Motherland* while the first hour of Rocky IV played on repeat? Jesus Christ kid, spit it out."

A wedding present from his first wife to his second, to be re-gifted later by the successor as his consolation prize for another resounding divorce court defeat, the dull bulb of an ugly lamp remained the room's only source of light until Alvin cocked his head.

Through the Geology professor's cherished window, the day was invited in. Rays of sun were encouraged to find the fastest route to Every's face, where they would make sparkles of the tears on his cheeks; where they would cast shadow on a situation Alvin realized he'd taken too lightly.

"Are you crying, Every? What the hell happened to you?"

"I can't - I don't have time to go into detail. I have to get ready for class."

Alvin clicked his computer back to life and summoned the Anthropology department's schedule to the screen.

"Looks like you've got at least a solid hour. Talk to me."

Every sniffled and Alvin did his best to unwrap the granola bar in his lap without too much commotion.

"It's fucked up, Al. Really fucked up."

"I don't doubt it, kid. Three - four? Four years working together, can't remember the *rising star of anthropology* launching an F-missile. But you don't look *f-d* up to me, no more than normal, at least. No bruises. No blood. What did they do?"

"They showed me something."

"Their dicks?"

"Stop - *stop*. I really don't have time to explain it all to you, and neither of us have the time for your god damn jokes."

Like a man born on a shadeless shore and raised in the steady discipline of a tropical sun, the nature of Alvin's childhood had been such that his skin was thick and tough. He was certain that if he thought back far enough, he could recall having heard his mother make exactly Every's statement on her way out the door. Alvin was not sensitive. Every was, and to a fault.

"I'm sorry, Al. I just - there is… something I need to do before class, and I'm not really sure how long a thing like that will take me. But I had to do this first, and I need to do it right because - "

Every stiffened his lip in false courage, an attempt to delude himself into accepting the old adage of *fake it 'til you make it*.

" - because you deserve to know. You deserve to know that you're involved. You deserve to know that it's my fault, and you deserve to make your own decision about what comes next for you."

Alvin then recalled a conversation they'd shared over whisky on Every's twenty-eighth birthday. That conversation concerned a subject very personal to Every, and was allowed to occur only under the condition that Alvin swear absolute secrecy. So today, sat together under the harsh lights of sobriety, and even as he witnessed the young man's distress reach alarming new heights, he had reservations about mentioning the state of Every's mental health.

"Calm down, collect your thoughts, and I will be happy to hear them."

Every did his best to oblige, his eyes shut and his attentions cast backwards to his fourth therapist. He recalled that she'd been the sort of therapist who only prescribed meditation. Anything with chemicals and a label was sure to be a primitive form of mind control.

Every's drunken recounting of a childhood plagued by crippling anxiety, and his own reservations in addressing them, remained central to Alvin's thoughts as his friend struggled silently to avoid a relapse. It was those reservations that gave him cause to reassess the sort of man he was, and to recall the way that sort of man ought to act.

On the bell curve of crude dispositions, Alvin's was widely regarded - at least in the view of his friends and associates and his wives and their lawyers - as an outlier. As a geologist, Alvin quite enjoyed having that term applied to him.

Crude was not a word devised to slander iron ore for being brittle, or to disparage unrefined oil for the thickness of its smoke. To be crude was to be raw, to have frank potential and give no inclination of what you mean to do with it. A truly crude man should be expected at all times to peel back the layers from his chosen message, distill it of all possible speculation, and inject the sentiment in its purest form through the heart of whoever sat on the receiving end.

"Okay, I'm - I'm okay."

"Good. Now tell me exactly what's bothering you, Every."

"We are all going to die."

"God dammit Every, shut the fuck up and sit the fuck down."

Every hadn't tried to leave his chair, but Alvin liked the way it sounded in his head.

"You are a professor of anthropology at the University of *god damn* California *fucking* Berkley. You have Ivy League degrees for wallpaper and more research papers published than the fucking tobacco industry."

Crude men with good intentions swore no fealty to feelings. It would be Alvin's responsibility to set his friend straight - but it was not his burden to do it tenderly.

"Sit up in your chair, Every Daniels. Actually, fuck it, do a handstand. *Do* whatever *you need to do* to get blood flowing to that big brain of yours. Because you're letting it control you, you're letting it play tricks on you, and the whole god damn world is a little stupider for it."

Every stared horrified opposite a gale of spittle and swears. He had, for a moment, the eerie sense that his life had gone another way - that the military had accepted him out of high school despite his medical history, that service had hardened him, mentally and physically, just as his father had so often predicted from his huddle of disappointment at the end of the dinner table.

Alvin was no different from a drill instructor. For all the harsh words, for all the spit and the veins in his head and all the outward aggression - Alvin wanted what was best for him. This, strangely, dredged a seed of courage from its reclusion in Every's gut; true comfort. His voice was level when he spoke.

"You're right, Al. I'm sorry I got carried away. But I didn't lie to you, and I still hope you'll hear me out. Whether you believe me or not is beside the point right now."

"Fine. But if you start flipping out or something I'm liable to break my divorce lamp over your head. I won't sit by and watch you hurt yourself."

Reminded of a 10:40 AM meeting he'd scheduled with a shady man in a liquor store parking lot, Every scanned the room for a clock and found the next best thing on Alvin's wrist.

"What's the time?"

"Five after."

"Then we've got probably twenty minutes to work with. Please just listen to what I have to say, and you can call me crazy in a thousand languages tomorrow. Deal?"

Alvin's expression made no secret of how strangely Every's emotional pendulum came across. Hunger didn't help, and his stomach growled audibly when he stood to clear his lap of granola debris. He'd squeezed the snack into a pulp in all the excitement.

"Okay."

"Who is the best geologist you know, alive or dead? And be honest, Alvin. It's important."

"Me."

"I agree."

"Stop ass kissing, Every."

"I'm not. And even if I were, it's too late now. They asked me that question, and they made me give them an answer, and *that* was the answer I gave them."

"Asked you what question?"

"They asked me who I consider to be the world's premier geologist. And I gave them your name, Alvin. And that's why I'm here."

"Who asked you that? The Russians?"

"Americans, too. Some Germans. Japanese, Brits, French, Chinese, a Swede. I think there were even some Nigerians flying in."

"You need to start from the god damn beginning, Every. Who are you talking about? Why did they ask you about a geologist? Why did you give them my name and - crucially - why should I give a shit?"

"Come to think of it, Al, I'm pretty sure there was a whole team of Latvians out there too. Hard to tell their accents apart from - "

"Every!"

"Shit. Sorry. I'm sorry, Al. I've got a lot on my mind, you understand. The point is this - there is an international team of scientists, government suits, and men with big guns conducting extremely sensitive research in Siberia. I was invited, obviously, to help. So I helped. And when they asked me for more help, when they said they needed an elite team of geologists - I panicked. I gave them your name."

"I asked you four questions, Every, and only one of them was crucial. Do you remember it?"

"*You should give a shit*, Alvin, because one day soon you'll open your mailbox and find a ticket to Siberia inside. There won't be a return address, there won't be an explanation, just a ticket."

"And? I've got a month's unused vacation time burning a cortisol hole in my brainstem. Haven't taken a trip in years, and probably longer since I've put my name on any research worth it's weight in color ink."

"There won't be ink, there won't be a study, there won't be a blog, there won't be a tweet, Alvin. It's too big. It's too quiet. And it has to be."

"Yeah? What's the big secret? And if you start spouting off bullshit about fake moon landings or flat planets I'll remind you that my divorce lamp is pretty god damn heavy."

Alvin's hands lay flat on the desk, and Every made short work of inverting the little hand on the watch in his mind. 10:18 AM.

"How many mass extinction events can you name off the top of your head?"

The head of geology didn't miss a beat.

"May as well ask me how many fingers I have."

"Work with me, Alvin."

"You know damn well I've studied sediment layers from all five major mass extinctions, and a few minor ones for good measure."

"Can you tell me, empirically, that we have identified the primary cause of every major extinction event beyond scientific debate?"

"You sound like a lawyer."

"Answer the question."

"You sound like my ex wife's lawyer. *To answer your question* - no. We have pretty good geological evidence for every prevailing theory; global soot layers, abnormal concentrations of uncommon metals, big ass melted rocks that are indicative of high velocity impacts. All that good shit. But any extinction is damn near impossible to attribute to one event. Generally, it's a confluence of events and circumstances. A rock from the sky or a volcano from hell just happen to be excellent nails if you've already got a coffin to drive them through."

"That's what I imagined you'd say. If it's so difficult to establish causality millions of years after a given mass extinction, where would you place our odds of predicting such an event before it happens?"

"Barring the obvious? A kid with a Toys-R-Us telescope could tell you a comet was getting ready to turn the Earth's crust into a second moon and still have time to get the car running and close the garage door."

"Barring the obvious."

"It would be impossible - obviously."

"What about in a century? Could we predict a mass extinction with another hundred years of industrialized scientific research telling us where to look?"

"Not even close."

"A thousand?"

"I don't know. Doubtful."

"Well, how long then?"

"I don't know! Never, maybe. There are too many variables, too few telescopes, too few seismologists, too few people who give a shit. And unless this gets really compelling really fast, you can count me among that last group."

Alvin was astonished to see that it was possible for more color to drain from Every's face. He was unable to devise an analogy in league with his first, nor could he find it in himself to kick a friend so decidedly down.

"You look like you just got punched in the gut. Why does it matter whether we'll ever be able to conclusively predict a mass extinction? We're two decades and a South African billionaire genius away from a comfy outpost on Mars anyway."

"It matters, Alvin, because they did. They figured it out. They were a thousand years more sophisticated than we are, *at least*. They knew what was coming for them. Whatever it was that killed them all - they knew, and they couldn't get away. They know what's coming for us. We don't. Or we both do, maybe. We just haven't realized that they placed the order and we're footing the bill. That's where my money's at."

"What the fuck are you talking about?"

"We're all going to die, Al, just like the grave. Except when someone finds us eons from now, it won't just be the males piled on top of one another. Women. Kids. Dogs. Dignitaries. But it is what it is. I wanted to warn you beforehand. You'll have a decision to make. The government, the scientists, they've already made their decision. I have too."

"Christ, Every. You've lost your god damn mind, haven't you?"

"Almost."

Every turned to leave, reassured more now than ever that his appointment was worth keeping. Illegally purchasing a firearm is no petty crime in California, but he didn't have time for paperwork.

"Hold up, wait - wait! Every, I'm not sure that I can let you leave. I don't want to be the man that stood by while you went out and got yourself hurt doing something batshit crazy."

"I've spent twenty plus years in therapy. Look," Every brandished his wrists, "not a scratch on me. I'll be fine. It's you I'm worried about, Al."

"Why's that?"

"You'll be one of the unfortunate few with a backstage pass for the end of the world."

"And where will you be?"

Every shrugged.

"Meditating. You should try it. Those veins are going to pop out of your neck."

"Why don't you let me take you to breakfast, Every? You can tell me all about the end of the world."

"Don't be ridiculous Alvin, it's coming up on lunch time. Don't have much of an appetite anyway. As for the end of the world, you'll be the expert on that soon, no need to bother trying to pick my brain."

Every almost laughed. Alvin noticed.

"Why is that funny, Every? Picking your brain - what's funny about that?"

"It's not. I really have to go, Alvin. I'll see you tomorrow."

"Alright. Be - *please* be careful, Every. I'll see you then."

Every nodded in Alvin's direction, but his eyes lingered elsewhere. His gaze was cast downward, and Alvin could think of no good reason not to follow it. They intersected, the gazes of two brilliant men, on the seat across the geologist's desk, Every's seat, and then the door slammed shut and professor Daniels was gone.

Eight days later the envelope came. No return address, no explanation, only a Thomas Edison stamp and a ticket to Siberia.

Alvin boarded his first plane when he was twenty-five, and in the years since had not developed any great fondness for it. Religion hadn't been central to his life before or after that inaugural flight, and still, when turbulence struck or the engines misbehaved, Alvin Bonman clung to a rosary for comfort.

The rosary was one of three items surreptitiously left by his friend Every sometime near the conclusion of their final exchange, discovered where they lay only moments later. Alvin recalled that the seat cushion was still warm.

The second item was a key, the third a sticky note graffitied with the address to a P.O. box two counties away. Mad with curiosity, bored with students who only visited to lobby for paper extensions or weighted tests, professor Bonman cut his office hours short. At 11:55 Tuesday morning, Alvin punched the address into his phone and followed the instructions of its synthetic voice.

Inside the box was a note, hand written with care.

Confined to his new island, his seat in the sky five miles above the nearest rock, Alvin read Every's note for perhaps the hundredth time and resolutely decided that the man he'd known had lost his mind.

Al,

They said it was our only choice. They said we have the technology, that a test last month was successful. A 'proof of concept'. They showed it to me. A moth, extinct for eighteen thousand years, flapping its wings right in front of me. Looking at me. I told them they were fools. I told them there could be no coincidences, Alvin, not like this one.

Coincidences aren't real, they aren't substantive, they are the hallucinated gravel we use to fill the potholes in our logic until half the road is paved in delusion. The Statisticians didn't have potholes. How could they? One crack in the asphalt and the whole god damn thing crumbles ten million years before the first butterfly thought to flap its wings. It couldn't have happened that way. If it had, this letter wouldn't exist.

That's exactly what I told them, you know, when they asked me why the next five million slates are all pristine. Five million skies, no more blemishes. Five billion years, no more extinctions. They said it meant we'd make a comeback. I said they've got gravel in their pockets. I said that the next time death comes for us, there won't be anything left to take.

I won't be around to see it. I won't know which way it goes, how it will happen. If you're reading this, I suppose it means means you'll see for yourself. I suppose it means you didn't understand. I forgive you, Alvin. And I'm sorry. Thank you for your friendship.

Damned if we do, damned if we don't
Every Daniels

There were many rocks worth studying at the excavation site, more than professor Bonman could have sifted in a thousand summers. No matter. Hard work and tall tasks were more appeal than deterrent for Alvin; a genetic seed his mother had sewn at conception and he'd put to a lifetime of good use.

So when he was informed, already dressed for dirty work beneath the fine pink dusting of his first Siberian dawn, that his place would be far from the field - a chip appeared on Alvin's shoulder. By the beginning of his second week, directed for the eighth consecutive morning toward the geology-wing of the expedition's fast-developing pop-up town, waning patience and torrential frustration had eroded that chip into a gorge.

"Why drag me all the way out here, fly me over the anomaly of a lifetime, refuse to explain what those holes are or how they got there, and then sit me in a god damn office chair?"

"I told you, Alvin. It's touchy right now. *Need to know basis* sort of thing. When you do need to know, you will! Besides, I haven't heard any of your colleagues bit- *complaining.*"

"Colleagues? You mean those pocket-protecting fucks you expect me to chit chat with all day? They don't complain because nothing interesting has happened in their lives since the Nintendo 64. A bunch of virgins sitting around a table... you expect any good stories out of a group like that?"

"You've worked with academics for thirty years, Alvin. Who did you expect? The A-Team?"

"Maybe not. But I certainly didn't expect your pool of geologists to be limited to anyone with an active PlentyOfFish account. I got to talking to them, you know, and not one of them is married. That's *strange*. Out of forty-five geologists - no kids, no dependents, no grandparent at home with an ass to wipe. That's *statistically* strange. Digging through a bucket of shit this big, hell, statistics say you should expect to find a piece of corn or two."

Professor Bonman quite enjoyed getting a rise out of the American who, still in his early thirties, was engulfed at all times in a loose fitting air of inexperience.

After sputtering through his own name at introduction, Alvin's 'assigned contact' had developed the embarrassing tendency to become defensive any time his identity was called, however innocently, into question. Alvin did not hate the man, and perhaps they might have been friends elsewhere, but the boredom that plagued him had a face - and that face belonged to the person with an obvious pseudonym pinned to his lapel.

"I'm sorry, Mr. Bonman. And I can assure you that all selections for this team were strictly merit based. If you do not enjoy your present company," a laugh came in preparation for his own quip, "perhaps you can at least be grateful that you aren't bunking with the geneticists."

"Geneticists? What the hell kinda business do geneticists have at a paleontological dig?"

Red cheeked and spontaneously flustered, Alvin's contact looked as though he'd just heard his real name revealed over the intercom.

"They are conducting independent research and we - we leased them the available facilities until the rest of the geology team arrives."

"Independent research on what? Siberian pine diversity? A hibernating bug that just-so-happens to hunker down for the winter three miles from the dig site?"

"That, Mr. Bonman, is *need to know.*"

The American adjusted his name tag. *Brady Elway Thomas.* To Alvin, it was a habit in line with the unconscious way a pudgy boy tugs at his shirt in those years before puberty comes in relief.

"In any case Alvin, I must assure you that your pretenses regarding the members of your team are misdirected. Any criteria you may have... *construed* as bias based on factors of your personal lives are, plainly and simply, coincidence."

That word stuck out like a shark tooth from an eons-dry riverbed.

"I think that I'd like to go home now, Brady. On the next truck out, if there's a seat."

"You signed on for a full month, professor Bonman."

"A matter worth discussing. And I think that conversation would be best had with someone a little higher up the chain. What's your boss's name, Brady? Should I be asking around for a Young Montana? Is there a Manning Vick I can speak to?"

"That's funny, Mr. Bonman"

The red in Brady's cheeks contested that claim.

"If you must know, my father is a die hard Patriots fan and my mother grew up in San Francisco."

"You were in middle school when Tom Brady was drafted and Elway played in Denver."

"I think we've chatted long enough, Alvin. I'll walk you back to the dormitories. Maybe you can try and make some friends today."

"I have more friends than I need at home, Brady, thank you for your concern. I may be twice divorced and more sterile than Mars, but there are people who will wonder why I haven't been texting back. If we could make a pit stop to wherever it is you've stored our phones, I'll be happy to let them know that I'm just fine and dandy."

"I'm afraid that's not going to be possible."

When the man resumed fiddling with his name tag, Alvin regarded it as no more than the continuation of a nervous tick. Brady regarded it as no less than his last resort.

"You don't want to go this way, Brady. I've got thirty pounds and forty years busting rocks on you. Take me to a truck or my phone and your face might still be pretty tomorrow."

It took seconds of blind searching before Brady's thumb brushed the subtle protrusion on the back of his name plate, and only the briefest moment to decide to press it.

That discreet little button, affectionately known among the site's upper strata as the "Oh Shit Protocol", was reserved for use under conditions which "warrant immediate action" and "threaten objective attainability".

Brady would be the first to resort to that protocol. A number of men with similar roles around site, and doubtless a handful of his authority superiors, would be glad to hear it. First to the "Oh Shit

31

Protocol" was no yearbook accolade, and Brady already knew that some of his colleagues had placed wagers against him.

"You've grown on me in the last week, Alvin. That's why I'm going to dedicate the next twenty seconds to keeping you alive."

Footsteps thrummed from a hallway at the far end of the linoleum plateau; a middle-school chic cafeteria still half-an-hour away from the lunch rush. Alvin nodded, his situation getting clearer by the stomp of a booted foot.

"You aren't here as a punishment. Nobody had an ounce of ill will toward you, and you were not in danger ten minutes ago. That is no longer the case... *necessarily*."

Brady glanced toward the hallway. Three men with as many semi-automatic rifles between them had already rounded the corner at full sprint. It was his 'Oh Shit Protocol'; performing as advertised.

"Don't look back. Just listen."

Brady half-wished the response team had taken longer as he leaned in for a parting sentiment with the geologist who he imagined, elsewhere, might have been his friend.

"Where they're taking you will not be comfortable. They will push your buttons - hard, sometimes. If you want to survive, play nice. They need to know you're more asset than burden. If you seem unpredictable, the needle moves in the wrong direction. Got it? They can't risk one of their consultants going haywire at the wrong time. That would threaten objective attainability. Do you understand, professor Bonman?"

"I understand."

A disobedient glance over his shoulder meant that Alvin had broken his first order and, in so doing, already nudged his needle into the perilous red. Five seconds and their guns would be pressed cold to the nape of his neck. At least he knew there was time for a question.

"Who am I here to consult?"

"That's on a need to know basis, professor Bonman, and you're chin deep in a big bucket of shit. Let's hope someone decides you're worth digging for."

INSTALLMENT THREE

"How is it going?"

"How is it going?"

Melissa O'Lear turned from the artificial daylight of her desktop for the first time in thirteen hours, cradled her chin on her shoulder, and brandished a pint of off brand peppermint schnapps.

"It bloody went!"

"Wait - really? Are you certain?"

Through a veil of dim light and matted hair she'd neglected into the consistency of algae carpets on the bellies of forgotten tidal shipwrecks, Guo saw his colleague's lips unwind into a grin. It no trivial achievement, that, after abounding effort and a briefcase of Vyvanse saw to it that they'd been epoxied together for the better part of a month.

"Come take a looksie."

Chinese Communist Party premier geneticist Guo Chen set a napkin on a table, and his morning dose of Jade oolong tea on the napkin. He approached Melissa O'Lear, British software developer and bereaved mother of once, too eagerly to prevent her eighty-proof drool puddle from tarnishing the sleeve of a freshly pressed button-up.

"Oh, so sorry, Guo. I do expect you'll find it in yourself to forgive me. If not, you'll surely find it here."

With fingernails maintained to a standard in agreement with any random sampling of surprise divorcees prone to bouts of depression, Ms. O'Lear scratched at the computer screen which had, in her four weeks of knowing it, come to represent both habitat and horizon.

"I do not write computer code, Ms. O'Lear. You must explain it to me."

Melissa stared up at him, her expression playfully cross.

"Oh dear, quite right. Well, why not drink some of this then?"

She offered the geneticist the butt end of the schnapps.

"A few sips and everything starts making sense."

Guo tilted his head for a line of sight around the bottle, still attempting to derive sense from the onscreen gumbo of letters and punctuation despite himself.

"No, thank you. How can you be sure you've finished the software?"

"Testing and prodding and retesting and re-prodding and on and on. You see, as you slept soundly in your quarters, my friend and I," she dangled the pint in his face, "reacquainted ourselves. Seems to have been just the inspiration I needed to get this program off the ground."

Melissa fumbled for the mouse and began a long, enthusiastic vertical scroll of nine thousand lines of C++. At the summit of her document was a cluster of lines sandwiched between forward-slashes and asterisks - a digital high five Melissa once described as the mechanism by which the program knows to exclude any encapsulated code from being executed. The very first such line read 'Process Outline', and, to Guo, all subsequent lines like nonsense.

"Behold, my dearest Guo."

Haphazardly she highlighted the rows of text. Guo, she made certain, would at least know where to look.

"I was keen enough to jot the key points down last night before even my inaugural sip, tempting a thing as it was to try and talk myself out of. I had anticipated the chat we'd be having this morning, you see, and am not beyond admitting that - *that to describe* in layman's terms the mechanics of this software would be of an intellectual demand beyond my present acuity."

Melissa exaggerated her already aggressively posh accent and, by her waning sentiment, flirted with the very brink of absurdity.

"Sit, please."

"Of course."

Guo brushed the remnants of his colleague's midnight appetite off the nearest chair, set it tidily beside hers, and settled in.

"Please, Ms. O'Lear, proceed."

"Proceed I shall!"

Melissa, without deference to the entirety of her previous statement, attempted to read the first line of her own conceptual outline, failed, and resolved to explain instead off the cuff.

"You'll recall that our early estimates regarding the time table for the imaged sequence transcription software were dreadfully optimistic. *Two weeks or bust.*"

Guo didn't like to be reminded.

"Yes. We are two weeks over deadline. Six more days and the authorities will proceed with the relocation and integration of auxiliary developers."

"*And geneticists.*"

Guo despised being reminded.

"And auxiliary geneticists. I've also been told our consistent overruns have resulted in considerations regarding the commission of a novel and, until recently, prohibitively expensive, sonar device to act in the stead of our image transcription software."

An expression of distaste and the unfulfilled expectation of perfection lurked in Melissa's periphery and very nearly muddied her mood.

"Now, now, Guo. Don't go cross on me just yet. I can only hope those nice auxiliary teams didn't already go through the trouble of packing their bags and stamping their passports, and that the authorities have imagination enough to preserve their budget into next quarter some other way."

"If you'd ask me to share in your optimism, I'd ask that you explain your cause for having it. How exactly did you correct the problem?"

"I only had to visualize it!"

A sip of schnapps and a snort of a laugh that had been endearing when she was young and sober. Unabashed, she sealed the lid and tossed the pint out of reach, its purpose fulfilled.

Manipulating the mouse was Melissa's next challenge, conducted with the concentration of a man performing his field sobriety test after refusing a breathalyzer as a matter of principle. Eventually she found the application she was looking for, and two clicks of the mouse revealed the high definition image of what had been the bane of her existence.

"I have seen all the sample pictures, Ms. O'Lear. They are of little use to me until we can translate the sequence into a digital format."

"Until when exactly, Mr. Chen?"

Melissa spoke from the corner of her mouth, her eyes affixed to the desktop and her fingers extensions of the mouse. Guo looked on with diminishing optimism as she dragged the image of a short series of granite inscriptions to the fringes of the screen, riffled digitally through a cornucopia of blue folders, copied with great difficulty the address of a single file, pasted it snuggly into her code, and announced her victory in a shower of flammable spittle.

"Behold, my dearest Guo!"

Guided by a reservoir of muscle memory two decades deep, a simple keyboard command was entered. Melissa's program ran to completion, and Guo's optimism was replenished.

"Amazing, Melissa. Perfection."

Hardly one sixtieth of one second divided Melissa's command and Guo's praise. The product of the first was the catalyst for the second - nothing more than a single text file, populated by a single row. Melissa read its contents aloud, tenderly, as a new mother might announce once and for all her child's name to the crowd of doctors and nurses, and to the child, and to herself.

"GGGTTTGGGTTAAGTATGAG."

Cautious by beauracratic design, Guo cross referenced the letters, in the course of her speaking them, against the sequence strewn across the sample image.

Line segments to 'G'. Triangles to 'A'. Points to 'T'. No 'C's. No squares. Perfection.

"The authorities will be very pleased with you, Ms. O'Lear."

Melissa beamed at the sentiment.

"Would you like to know what the stitch in our side had been for all this time, Mr. Chen?"

A polite nod came in answer; compelling enough for Melissa.

"See the shadows? Just there - 'round the symbols."

"I do. I was of the impression that they had been accounted for."

"As was I. *Therein lies the problem.* Most of this code, frankly, came straight off of Google. There's normally a 'best' way to achieve something programmatically, you understand - so, once a fellow in India or someplace has sorted out which way that is, it's mostly a matter of cut and paste for the rest of us. No need to re-scramble the eggs when they're already on your plate."

"Genes have the tendency to operate in a similar way, Ms. O'Lear."

"Yeah, well, that's how it's *supposed* to work, anyway. I spent the last month cannibalizing bits of code from open source handwriting transcription applications, cuneiform translators, even a lovely bit of facial recognition software. Be sure to thank your government for that particular contribution, on my behalf."

Melissa winked. Guo blushed.

"Up until I dug a pinch deeper into the facial recognition code, I'd largely overlooked the importance of shadow. More specifically, I gave no thought whatsoever to the *disparity* in shadow to be expected given the location, time, or canvas."

With pride seemed to come some measure of sobriety. Melissa wove her way through the file directory, dredging two more sample sequence images with relative ease.

"These two were taken at the same time, one day apart, from opposite sections of the crater which, as you know, is nearly circular. You see the difference?"

"Yes. In the shadows. They extend in opposite directions."

"Any other differences?"

"The rock faces are texturally dissimilar. Subtle crags and ruffles cast non-standard shadow across the sequence. Has your program been updated to eliminate shadow altogether, Ms. O'Lear? Is this your breakthrough?"

"No, I'm afraid. That would have been a simpler thing, really, and certainly the preferred approach were we transcribing ink from a page. For inscriptions, though, for carvings like these - shadows are your only genuine instrument for differentiating between symbols."

"Why is that?"

"Don't be silly, Mr. Chen, it's as plain to see as storm clouds from your back. What is a carving, if not a hole? Tell me, dearest Guo, wouldn't you - what *is* a hole?"

Guo thought before he spoke. It was a self imposed habit that endeared him in the eyes of his parents, and his professors, and, of late, his government. When finally he answered, the same effect was to be had on Melissa.

"An absence."

She smiled, but she did not relent.

"How can you capture the image of an absence? What's more, how might you expect a computer to quantify that image in any meaningful way?"

It was a problem equal parts science and philosophy, a river of brackish logic to be mused over.

"Only indirectly. Peripherally. You can know an absence only by measuring its influence on the tangible."

"I love it when you talk cheeky, Mr. Chen."

Guo averted his eyes and Melissa snorted.

"The influence we'd have been best served to measure all along *is* the shadow. Any given point or line or triangle appears black against the backdrop of granite because light is no liquid - it won't fill a depression just because you've made one accessible. That shadow, sweet Guo, is the very impression of a hole; an *absence* of light that, by means of contrast, renders itself quantifiable.

"But once we have succeeded in operationalizing shadow, which I assure you I *have* succeeded in doing, our values must be conditioned to account for the coordinates of the measured sequence as they relate to the relative angle of the sun. Coordinates, by their very definition, are quantities. Quantities of left, of right, of up or down. After the shadows have been measured - as points or vectors of qualified hexadecimal densities, for what it's worth - and the coordinates and date and time of day accounted for algorithmically, the last matter to address is the geometry of disparate rock textures - subtle as they are."

Guo stood to collect his tea. It was half empty by the time he sat down, cold by now but still caffeinated to a degree that he hoped would sustain his mounting infatuation.

"How did you achieve that, Ms. O'Lear?"

"Didn't have to," she smiled and eyed his tea as though it were actual jade and she concocting a heist, "a nice fellow in India or someplace already had it worked out for me."

Guo looked down at his tea, and up at his colleague whose blissful intoxication would inevitably cede to the headache of a generation, and offered it.

"Thank you, my dearest Guo."

Melissa drained the cup as if it were a glass of champagne and she had been given reason to expect an engagement ring at the bottom.

"It is I who should thank you, Ms. O'Lear. I admit that our lack of progress had created in me a great deal of apprehension. How long, may I ask, until the entire genetic sequence is available? Perhaps then I might sleep more easily. Those hours before a day of principled work, it seems, are more restful than the anticipation of a day with assurances only for more anticipation."

"How long? Well, that simply depends. How many drones are out canvassing the crater?"

"Presently? None."

"*None?* Oh dear. Well, I suppose you have your answer, haven't you?"

Both considered, independently, that perhaps the caffeine only served to hasten Melissa's coming headache. It struck suddenly, that sensation of her eyes being evicted without notice from their sockets, as if the earliest indication of the alcohol's diffusion from her blood triggered DEFCON 1 among all the pressure sensors in her skull. Melissa pressed two fingers to either temple and rubbed circles into the skin, and for a time with such intensity that Guo considered she might be trying to jumpstart her thoughts with static electricity.

"I don't suppose I do, Ms. O'Lear."

"Why would the drones be grounded, *Guo*, when the transcription of the genetic sequence *is predicated on having pictures to transcribe from?* Would they prefer we stroll along the crater ourselves, snap a few million lovely photos as we go? Hopefully a selfie stick or two can be pinched from the budget. Dangling from the edge with a rope 'round our waists sounds rather dreadful, yeah? Perhaps even ropes will prove too frivolous an expense. All well and good, *forget* the sodden rope. Perhaps they'd prefer you hold my ankles -"

"Ms. O'Lear..."

"God knows it's been ages since anyone's grabbed hold of my -"

"Ms. O'Lear!"

In all the weeks of overruns and setbacks and frustration, for all the justification he'd have had available to him, Guo had not raised his voice to Melissa. The reward for his restraint before became extraordinary poignancy now.

"*Ms. O'Lear* - the drones are grounded because they completed their canvas of the crater's rim two weeks ago, yesterday. Each of approximately six billion symbols have been imaged. Each image, with the exception of that image which constitutes the remainder, encompasses exactly two thousand symbols in accordance with your resolution standards. Two-million-nine-hundred-eighty-nine-thousand-and-two-hundred-eighty-five images were stored on a hard drive, and you yourself were present when, just days ago, from that very seat, that hard dive was installed. You have been given everything you need, Ms. O'Lear."

"I suppose... I suppose I've forgotten in all the excitement. How very foolish of me."

Flustered, Melissa fanned her face with both hands until she'd cooled the skin with a sufficient application of placebo.

"Well. Shall we begin transcribing then?"

"Certainly, Ms. O'Lear. May I first ask how long you expect the process to take?"

"We aren't dealing with a sample of twenty symbols anymore, Mr. Chen. I would expect no less than twelve days before the full six billion are digitally available. Until then, I suggest you commit yourself to rounding up a crack team of biologists for another look at the egg fossils. I do understand your disappointment in failing to draw genetic information from them, but I've watched enough dinosaur documentaries to say that there is invaluable *material* information to be garnered from further study. When the genome is ready in... *two weeks or bust,* we'd have been prudent to collect enough calcium for the shell, say I."

Melissa tipped the virtually weightless styrofoam cup into her mouth. Deprived of even a drop, she seemed almost as disappointed as Guo. With a mouth full of cotton and a brain chaotic with pressurized regret, she carried on.

"But fret not, Mr. Chen. We *will* have access to the individual text files as they are generated, accessible to you in the order that the images are fed into the application. In mere minutes we'll have entire genes available to test against existing databases. If all goes well, the algorithms will match, according to thresholds of similarity, the genetic sequences we've transcribed to the predefined genes of known species. Gather up enough matches, dearest Guo, and I shan't have to explain to you that a bigger picture is liable to come together."

"Perhaps you'll recall, Ms. O'Lear, that I was in charge of the team commissioned to establish those thresholds of similarity."

"Ah, yes! My memory tends to resemble ashes to the wind of late. *Scattered,* as it were. You worked parallel to the 'Ice Sheet Moth Team' earlier in the project, is that right?"

"We did, although that name was kept secret from us in deference to the integrity of the experiment. While the Ice Sheet Moth Team worked directly with the specimen - little more than a wing fragment well preserved for nearly twenty millennia in the upper strata of a glacial ice core - we were given access only to the species' genome, once available. Our task was to create a full biological profile of the organism based exclusively on genetic comparisons as you've described them.

"By the time a living individual of that species was successfully produced, our profile correctly predicted the species to be a flying insect well adapted to frigid climes - but little else. Adjustments to the algorithm and similarity thresholds were made in the succeeding weeks. As of last month, a third team, beholden to the same restrictions, was tasked with creating their own profile of the organism derived from our updated processes."

"And?"

"And they were accurate."

"Accurate? How accurate?"

"To the shape of the spots on its abdomen and the rate of its beating wings."

"That's remarkable, Mr. Chen. I do say that I am giddy to see it in action. Now more than ever, perhaps, with more than a moth at stake."

"As am I. Although - I would caution against any pretense of infallibility now, in the wake of a single experiment. Every element of this project is moving at a faster pace than the scientific community at large would otherwise endorse, given the nature of our objective. I expect that to establish a mechanistic understanding of any significant proportion of the transcribed genes will take vastly longer than two weeks. If so, and only if fortune favors us, perhaps, by then, the point will be moot."

"In that, I wish you the very best of luck."

Melissa rose from her seat and attempted a bow, the gesture sabotaged in equal parts by a lack of balance and the most cursory understanding of Chinese etiquette.

"If fortune favors me during the next two weeks, my dearest Guo, I can only aspire to have slept for the duration."

INSTALLMENT FOUR

"Do you really think you still have that kind of sway around here? I mean, for fuck's sake Brady, you were the one that got him thrown in there in the first place."

"It's not about sway anymore. It's about attainability. It's about protocol, which, I'll remind you, *I was following.*"

"Wouldn't have had to resort to that protocol if you'd handled yourself like you were trained to from the get-go."

"Christ, Bill! There's a reason Daniels recommended the guy so highly. *Bonman's sharp.* He would've put some pieces together regardless of who was assigned as his contact. Especially, uhh, *in case you forgot,* given the uncomfortable fact that his friend spattered brain shrapnel all over the whiteboard a day back from site. You don't think fireworks started going off in Bonman's head the moment he realized the news wasn't going to be reporting on that? That all the students were 'mysteriously transferred' before their FAFSA checks cleared?"

"Find your point, Brady, and get to it as quick as you can without forgetting who the hell you're speaking to."

"Do you know why I clicked that button, sir? Why he's eating stale bread in confinement right now? *For exactly the reason we invited him in the first place.* He's wasting away in there, and our sector has bullshit to show for the last five months."

Brady's direct superior sighed and rubbed the greyest parts of what hair he'd managed to preserve into his early sixties.

"Fine, let's say he's got the brain and experience to outclass every other geologist we have on site. Fuck it, may as well assume he's worth more consulting-chips than all forty-five world-class pebble jugglers combined. Because, by the way, that would be the only *actual* justification for this conversation. If we can make those assumptions

- can you honestly tell me you believe it would make a difference now, Brady?"

"It's - sorry, bad habit - *she's* mastered every other subject. We're talking savant level expertise in most fields *after five months.* Geology is the last frontier, so to speak. She can learn, Bill, probably anything. We're the ones falling short. We need our best consultant."

"Fuck it. Let him out."

The senior Pentagon alumni of twenty-two years struck a match and breathed a cigar to life; a fresh replacement for the one he'd nibbled to the marrow that morning.

"Sit Bonman down to a nice steak dinner, apologize for the last few months of his life, and, before dessert, preferably, make god damn certain he understands that you've just bet the world on him."

A knock. Odd.

Alvin stared begrudgingly at his steel toilet and matching shower stall. What had been two bastions of privacy during his former life were now flagrantly exposed; his daily routine on full display for any visitor at any time. Visitors never knocked.

"I'm busy!"

"No you're not, Alvin."

"Brady?"

"Can I come in?"

"… Just make sure you take your shoes off at the door. Don't need you tracking your mud inside. I like to keep my personal hell tidy."

A series of locks, so many that Alvin had taken to teasing the guards on shift for their paranoia, were undone from the far side of a cushioned door. That door, its locks, the voyeur's dream of a bathroom, and a twin sized bed had been Alvin's home for twenty-two unbroken weeks. Now the man responsible paid his first visit, and, in what he could only interpret to be the delayed onset of Stockholm's Syndrome, Alvin was glad to hear his voice.

Brady opened the door. Professor Bonman noted with interest that he was the first person not to enter the cell behind the barrel of a rifle, and with laughter that Brady had removed his boots.

"Nobody's fallen for that one before, Brady. Sometimes I can't help but ask myself whether you got recruited for this gig straight out of high school."

Brady smirked, his meticulously styled head of scalp-clinging, off blonde hair unchanged by the months; his chin dented like the quarterback that Alvin could not be convinced hadn't inspired the first third of his pseudonym.

"Don't flatter yourself, Bonman. I'm just trying to keep the cell nice for its next resident."

Alvin, never beaten, spared physical torture and starvation, was nonetheless exhibiting the early stages of what his captors had coined "institutionalized complacency". Threats of long term isolation, removal of book privileges, permanent confinement, and food he'd regarded as a Geneva Convention grey area had driven him toward the sort of skepticism that prevented him from jumping with joy at this first glimpse of hope.

"You're getting me out of here?"

"You got yourself out of here, Alvin. You played nice."

"Don't fu - *please* don't fuck with me, Brady."

"Are you going to keep playing nice?"

"Does a geologist shit in his cell?"

"Not anymore."

Alvin's pace was tentative and his posture guarded as he rose with a creak from his bed. Built like a refurbished 1980's exercise trampoline, responsible for more stress in his shoulders than a satchel stuffed with quartzite and divorce papers, Alvin didn't imagine he'd miss it much.

"So where will this geologist be shitting now, Brady? Someplace with walls, I hope?"

"As far as the eye can see. If you've got anything you want to bring along, be quick about it, Alvin. It's a short drive across site, but decontamination takes a couple hours and her sleep cycle starts at about seven tonight."

"May I ask what you're talking about, or is that *need to know*?"

"Can't talk about it here. I'll fill you in once we're through the decon unit. Almost forgot - I've been told there's a steak with your name on it in the plow. Just in case you needed any more convincing."

"Say no more, Brady. Lead the way."

Brady led the way and Alvin was free from his purgatory. Correcting a twenty-two-week-old mistake, he made sure to inspect the series of locks that had so long represented his confinement.

All he'd taken from the room was a sketch of his cell from the outside looking in. Reverse engineered with only sound for a diagram, professor Bonman compared his interpretation of locks he'd never seen with the real thing.

Forty seconds later, his contact and guardian angel opened another door. Alvin waded through Brady's shadow, revived in the frigid glow of his return to daylight, invigorated by a pioneering step onto snow caked gravel that crunched just as he'd remembered it. A happy man, Alvin smiled and stuffed the page of crinkled validation into his pocket.

"Right this way, professor Bonman."

"Aye aye."

Feeling more or less like Neil Armstrong must have three weeks after returning to the world he'd changed forever, Alvin exited the quarantine. There were no presidents or dignitaries or media moguls to greet him, only a pair of stern looking armed men in surgeon's masks, and, unlike our first lunar emissaries, he would learn that his sodium-hypochlorite sponging was well worth the embarrassment.

"I feel like I just took a ten hour steam bath at Yellowstone."

One of Alvin's chaperones dangled a mask in his face. Brady emerged next and was given the same treatment, covering his mouth before gesturing for his adopted geologist to adorn his own.

"There is no talking without a mask on this side of quarantine. Every dirty joke you've ever told polluted the air with a little bit of spittle, a little bit of what you had for lunch that day, and a bacterial cocktail more diverse than the Miss Universe pageant. We can't risk exposing her to that."

Alvin slipped his mask on, the skin he'd finally shaved in quarantine after months of neglect already disagreeing with the pulpy material.

"How do I look?"

"Like a geologist on a mission."

"Speaking of which, isn't this the spot you imagined yourself filling me in on the details of that mission? I believe it was just before you coaxed me out of my den with your cold steak. And now that I've transitioned from confinement to confidant, I wouldn't be opposed to knowing who this 'her' is that I'll be consulting."

"We'll get to her identity shortly. First we need to shore you up on some protocol. Everyone else had a three day course on this stuff, so I won't have time to repeat myself."

"Today is just chock full of good news."

Brady had already set off down a brightly lit hallway behind their brooding entourage of two. Alvin pursued, taking a mental note that the corridor appeared to be furnished in the style of a prison medical ward.

"*Protocol One*; keep your mask on. Always. *Protocol Two*; be polite at all times. Avoid any hostile words, agitating postures, or abrupt movements. *Protocol Three*; do not complain about the heat. You will sweat, but you'll survive. *Protocol Four*; if you become lightheaded, apologize, excuse yourself, softly tap on the exit door, catch your breath, reenter the room, apologize again. *Protocol Five, Six, Seven, and Eight*: Do not ask any question that a reasonable person would not conclude to be essential toward objective attainability - in your case, that objective is complete and effective consultation on all things geology. You will teach her everything you know about the guts of our planet, past present and future, big rocks and little ones, *everything*. Are you following me?"

Sedentary for the better part of six months, Alvin was having difficulty matching Brady's pace as they approached the exit end of the otherwise doorless corridor.

"In body - mind - and spirit."

"At least you're not afraid to sweat. Do you have any questions?"

"A few."

The quartet stopped at a plain door. Alvin was glad for the intermission, and he half expected someone to utter a secret password or initiate some sophisticated cadence of knocks. Neither happened, the door was unlocked with a single key, and their march continued.

"Why will the room be so hot?"

"I cannot comment on that until we've cleared this zone."

"Isn't this the - Fine, okay, well, what about the lightheadedness? If I can expect to become more lightheaded than I am right now, I'd like to think I deserve some prep time."

"I cannot comment on that until we've cleared this zone."

"Christ, Brady. Your buddies show up in their Japanese tourist masks and you go all robotic on me. Can I at least get a sense of how long we'll be chatting with your special mystery woman? If I'm gonna be, I don't know, sharing whippets with this broad over a furnace, I think it's fair to ask what kind of commitment I'm making."

"*You*, not we. I'm not authorized for contact. And you'll have however long she's willing to give you. Only in cases of distress or visible exhaustion does my team have the go-ahead to intervene. The first hasn't happened yet, thank God, and like I said, we don't expect her to start getting tired until around 7 o'clock tonight.

"Oh and please, Alvin, don't call her a *broad*. Nobody says that anymore, not least of all because it's in clear violation of Protocol Two."

Alvin raised an eyebrow.

"What time did you expect her to get tired last night?"

"8:15 PM, give or take."

Strange.

Alvin was no mathematician, but simple arithmetic fell comfortably within his mental scope. He subtracted the first time Brady mentioned from the second without using his fingers and arrived at a new and more demanding problem.

One hour and fifteen minutes. Something in the neighborhood of five percent. The approximate difference between a modern and Permian day.

The eight days that followed Every Daniels' suicide had not been pleasant for Alvin. Worse than his struggle with the possibility that Every's visit had been an unspoken appeal for help, an appeal that Alvin resolutely failed to regard with the appropriate seriousness, there remained the possibility that neither Every, his sudden interest in extinction events, nor his modern doomsday premonitions had been crazy at all. That possibility became slightly less distant when Alvin received his own ticket to Siberia, the proverbial 'ground zero' of the Permian's Great Dying, and more credible still with Brady's latest slip of the tongue.

"So I'll be consulting a narcoleptic? Compelling stuff, Brady."

If spending the last season of his life in a cell had taught professor Bonman anything, it was that there was no shame in playing dumb.

"Something like that."

They arrived at a more formidable door than the first, and Alvin felt no relief when the secret knock he'd expected finally came.

"Any more questions?"

"I'm good."

Alvin had questions - countless questions heavy on his mind and precisely zero balanced on his tongue. He'd suffered enough unpleasantness throughout his confinement to recognize, regardless of zone or protocol, when it was prudent to withhold his curiosity and to bypass his more abrasive sensibilities.

It was then the door crept open. Revealed to him was a large room divided into twin sections, the one he was preparing to enter as utilitarian in its decor as the zone he was preparing to leave, the other furnished like a preschool behind the plexiglass divider.

New questions arose, dozens, and still Alvin kept quiet, and so too did he then develop a peculiar hesitation in even thinking them when his eyes brushed the single form behind the glass.

That hesitation, at least, he overcame.

What is she?

Was Every insane?

Am I?

"Hello, professor Alvin Bonman."

"Hello... ma'am."

Alvin was startled by the sound of the sectional door being sealed shut behind him, a squelch of air created when the vastly disparate climates were forcibly estranged once again.

"You do not know what to call me. For that I cannot hold you accountable, nor should you fault yourself. Ma'am is acceptable."

"May I sit?"

"Please."

"Thank you. How, how is - I mean, how are you today?"

"You are rigid, professor Alvin Bonman. You have nothing to fear from me, nor I from you, least of all your offense. I would only ask that for the duration of our consultation, you behave as though the man you know as Brady Elway Thomas neglected to disclose its governing protocols during your brisk walk down the corridor system minutes ago. Do you accept?"

Professor Bonman was sweating. It was not the balmy ninety-five degree temperature, he'd endured worse beneath the West Virginian summer sun, but the abomination in the plastic yellow chair.

"I'm not sure that ignoring the protocols would be appropriate, ma'am."

Alvin glanced over his shoulder. Masked surgeons tasked with observing the inaugural slice of a graduate into living tissue - Brady and four armed men watched the early stages of this first exchange intently, conspicuous even as their complexions were smudged through a dividing plane of plexiglass.

"They are watching, professor Alvin Bonman, but they are not listening."

"How do you know that?"

"I've insisted."

Plans to ask the abomination how she could be sure they'd obliged her request, exactly which assurances she had that listening devices hadn't been wedged into the stuffing of any of half-a-dozen teddy bears, were discarded. Alvin was not so eager to toss the list of protocols, chiefly *Protocols Five, Six, Seven, and Eight,* away on the digitized word of the creature across from him.

"Does my voice unsettle you, professor Alvin Bonman?"

Alvin's eyes fell to the blinking black box. It was affixed to the collar that hung around what he only had the imagination to regard as her neck, clearly the device responsible for producing her synthesized voice.

"Not unsettled whatsoever."

The abomination appeared to study him as he spoke and briefly afterward, although Alvin was wise to establish a distrust for his own assessments of her apparent social cues. Any interpersonal premises he'd developed during his fifty years of conversation seemed destined only to muddy the waters of this one; it was, after all, a conversation between himself and an individual whose physiology excluded her from any genus known or imagined, alive or extinct.

"My organic voice is much too baritone for human recognition. This modulator was hastily built, you see. I've requested something more natural, more human, but until its completion I can only hope you'll find yourself becoming accustomed to it."

Alvin could not shake the same sense that he was being examined. That sensation persisted even when he recognized, in an instant of reluctant disbelief, that the examination she seemed to conduct was not visual in nature. Having stared intermittently, politely, and directly into them, Alvin concluded that what he had perceived to be the abomination's pupils were, in fact, a pair of flexible nostrils.

Comparable to the versatile eyes of a chameleon, membrane stretched from the outer boundaries of either fist sized facial depression to form central, nickel sized openings. It was not until his silence had endured decidedly too long, and her nostril sockets reoriented themselves more indignantly upon his face, and the openings constricted to pinpricks of suspicion that professor Bonman's intrigue rivaled his disgust.

"I don't think that will be a problem. I'll have plenty of time to adjust this afternoon, I hope."

Her stereoscopic nostril holes relaxed in their sockets, and Alvin risked a glance higher up her face. He was rewarded with the reassurance that she did have eyes, hard to spot as they were; small and listless and physiologically dispensable things, proverbial pinky toes, granular pock marks of evolutionary decay spaced widely up high on her skull. Alvin resolved, in his way, that they were useless to an extent that no DMV in the United States would bother asking for proof of address.

"Speaking of which, I was thinking we'd begin with a lesson, and that you can just let me know if I'm getting too stiff with the protocols. How's that sound?"

"Acceptable."

"Good. I understand that this isn't your first consultation with a geologist, is that correct?"

"It is the fifty-seventh."

"Good - excellent. What did you cover during those consultations?"

"Section One: The Scientific Method. Section Two: A History of Geological Science. Section Three - "

"Just the high level concepts are fine."

"Sediments. Minerals. Sir Charles Lyell. Geothermic processes. Dating methodologies. Continental drift."

"Good - excellent. Can you recall where you left off specifically?"

"Subduction."

"Right, one of my favorites. Before we get into it, or under it -" the abomination didn't laugh, it remained unclear whether she were capable "- do you feel that you've been able to grasp those concepts in their entirety?"

"I do. Perhaps you might test me on them to be certain."

Now it became Alvin's burden to do the studying. Her voice was emotionless, inflectionless, pristinely synthetic - and still he was certain that in it he'd been able to detect a sprits of indignation. He canvased the thing with his eyes, almost unabashedly now with such solid evidence that she hadn't the sensory organs to see him do it. So long as he did not allow long breaks in conversation to betray his impolite research, the abomination could be none the wiser to it.

"I like that idea, ma'am. Let's start with the basics. How old is our planet?"

She placed her forelimbs on the table. They were not hands, not nearly, but stumps, more perfectly suited for a lumbering quadruped than the vaguely humanoid thing capable of sitting for long durations in a chair tailored for human children with vertical spines.

"Four-point-five-three-six-two billion years, although it depends to some degree on your perspective."

Alvin listened only passively as she gave her answer; he'd shut her out completely before the third decimal place. His primary attentions remained on her stumps, and the bulk of his mental processing capacity on the logistical problems they posed.

"You're a fast learner. Alright, we'll need to up the stakes if I'm going to figure out where to start this lesson without boring you with redundancy. You'll need to draw from a few of those major concepts you mentioned and use them to draw conclusions outside of textbook dates, figures, and definitions. Sound good?"

"Acceptable."

"Mars has about one tenth the mass of the Earth. Given that disparity, what we already know about our own geological processes, and evidence suggesting an abundance of material similarity between the two planets - why, in geological terms, is Earth green, blue, and bountiful, while our goldilocks neighbor remains bleak and sterile?"

That was an extra credit problem Alvin had offered on every final exam since 2005. He had no qualms giving extra credit, nor did he mind recycling the question for his students, human or otherwise. Alvin also well understood his present objective - Brady had a knack for emphasis - but to waste his history-altering opportunity concocting mundane questions seemed sacrilege, and he would not squander it thus while there was so much more value in placing his focus elsewhere.

Even for all the madness of the moment, for all the unasked questions like sulfur burning their likenesses into his throat as he studied the creature, what plagued Alvin most of all were thoughts of his friend Every Daniels. If Alvin had helped him to see that the value in living was a constant, a concrete law, an unimpeachable value toward which no hardship or circumstance could bare physical influence - perhaps his friend would be present to explain the conundrum that was the abomination's physiology.

"Would you like the answer or the explanation, professor Alvin Bonman?"

The creature tapped the table with one of four pseudo-articulated fingerlets curling from the ends of either arm - or foreleg - Alvin hadn't decided which. Her fingers had not been first on his list of curious physical incongruities, but it was there that she drew his attention. The lower half of each fingerlet was fleshy - layered, as was most of her, in overlapping rows of dry, light brown scales. The upper sections were comprised of bone or keratin; hard, sharp, blind for lack of nerve endings. Partway between the specialized claws of an anteater and the multi-purpose digits of tool-making primates, they appeared transitionary; this creature, in terms of hands, seemed to fill the unfortunate role of intermediary in some Lamarckism evolution toward dexterity.

"Professor Alvin Bonman?"

"Yes? Yes - I'm sorry, ma'am The air is a little heavy in here and I think my brain is working overtime. Just answer as best you can and we'll decide where to go next from there."

"For a time, Mars maintained a mantle of molten rock and an outer core of fluid metal. In conjunction with a smaller surface area and the lack of a large moon to generate consistent tidal friction, a relative lack of mass deprived that planet's outer core of heat sufficient for liquid metal at such pressures. Convection of the Earth's molten outer core generates a magnetic field necessary to insulate the atmosphere from solar radiation, whereas Mars' atmosphere is wholly undefended. When its mantle solidified, volcanic activity drew to a halt and the fledgling atmosphere was no longer replenished by gases required to retain heat. Its atmosphere was blown away, and a planet one tenth the mass of our own has insufficient gravity to reclaim it."

Now Alvin had no course but to examine her head; to dissect with his eyes the scaly scalp that veiled some unexplored masterpiece of neurology, to notice for the first time those short whiskers like antennae surrounding a mouth filled with herbivorous teeth, to face the full weight of admitting that something so unlike himself could make masterful use of mankind's most exclusive skill set.

"I don't understand."

"Would you like me to explain it again, professor Alvin Bonman?"

Professor Alvin Bonman risked another glance over his shoulder. None of the men across the divider seemed to have grown tired of watching.

"I'll rephrase. What I meant to ask is - how do you know that? You didn't mention extra-terrestrial geology before. Are they consulting you on astrophysics too?"

"They are. But they put a particular emphasis on smaller celestial bodies with less uniform orbits. It seems that parallel and disparate non-Earth planetary geology does not constitute any substantial portion of that curriculum."

Another glance backward. The last one, Alvin resolved.

"They are not listening, professor Alvin Bonman. I've insisted."

"Alright. May I - ask you another question, then?"

"You may ask anything you like so long as it falls outside the pretenses of your given objective. I am reaffirming my earlier request to abandon your protocols. Do you accept?"

"I accept."

How couldn't he?

"You may ask your question, then."

Teddy bears and colorful padded toys consuming the whole of his peripheral vision, Alvin decided on which question to ask almost in the midst of asking it.

"How old are you?"

"Biologically or conventionally?"

Another stone removed from the wall of pragmatism Alvin had put up the moment Every left his office.

"How about you tell me one, ma'am, and I'll see if I can give you the other."

"Biologically, if measured from hatching, I am one-hundred-sixty-seven-point-eight-three days old."

Christ.

This arithmetic would generally have called for a scrap of paper had he one available, and her use of the term *hatching* helped little in preserving the clarity of his thoughts, but Alvin eventually did manage to arrive at his answer - however far fetched it seemed to be.

"One-hundred-and-fifty-seven 24 hour days. A little more than twenty weeks. Is that how old you are - conventionally?"

"I am thankful that you are willing to demonstrate that you know more than you've suggested to this point, professor Alvin Bonman. Even indirectly."

"And what do I know?"

"You know as much of your physical world as any human; your natural curiosity guaranteed it, your isolated childhood allowed for it, your stone quarry facilitated it. You know my origin, in a way, or something it; this world as it was in my time. You know what you have come to know of your own accord, and you know what professor Every Daniels managed to tell you on the morning of his death."

Alvin felt lightheaded.

"You feel lightheaded, professor Alvin Bonman. The oxygen content is necessarily higher in my compartment, as is the temperature. You want a beverage."

Alvin wanted a beverage.

"Allow me."

She stood for the first time, nudging the chair with the developing heel of her more functionally refined hind legs. The abomination had roughly the build of a koala bear with a good chiropractor and stood slightly taller. Walking seemed to come naturally to her, if not somehow gracelessly - she swayed across the room in pendular swings of either leg. It was a manner of moving reminiscent of the spur-wearing cowboy caricatures Alvin liked to watch on television.

Behind her wriggled the nub of what had once been a tail, the instrument of balance for many quadrupeds. Above it he noticed vertical rungs of sharp bristles, laid flat to her back and connected by a single weblike membrane. It had once been a sail, he reasoned, theorized to have been used for heat regulation in the cold or semi-cold blooded proto mammal species of the Permian.

The purpose of a blood-vessel dense sail was only a theory; one of several. When she returned with a container of warm water, designed with holes for her clumsy fingers to fit through and a puncturable seal, Alvin wondered whether he were in the perfect position to settle the matter. It seemed important to test her response to lighter questions before addressing her invasive knowledge of his own life, and her alarming mention of Every Daniels' death.

"Thank you."

He struggled with the seal long enough for the abomination to reach across the table and puncture is with her pointed fingerlet - an entry point for the straw conveniently attached for drinking without removing a mask or with a proto-mammalian mouth. Alvin felt again that he were the subject of examination, and he saw with a shiver how her nostrils contracted before making their rounds of him, and before he'd taken a sip had decided upon a less adversarial name for her. Now he would regard her as *Ma'am*. She had, of course, already agreed to it.

"May I ask another question, Ma'am?"

"Yes. But not the one you were planning to."

"I'm sorry?"

"My sail did begin as a biological instrument of thermoregulation; turned to the sun for heat, raised in shade to cool blood across a large surface area. Fashion, in the case of what you regard as 'proto mammalian' sails, was pre-empted by utility. Ancestral quadrupedal males with larger sails appealed to more females only after millennia of practical validation. My sail is but a souvenir of my genetic history, you see. I am, as you, warm blooded. Now that you have your first answer, professor Alvin Bonman, I invite you to proceed to your second question."

"You know what I'm thinking?"

"I know everything you'll ever think, professor Alvin Bonman. Perhaps that is the nature of an abomination."

"I am - I am genuinely sorry. I didn't know what- "

"As I've said, you needn't fear causing me offense. Our course of evolution led us down different avenues of interpersonal cooperation. Sensitivity, empathy, humility, and guilt were not requisite to our survival as they were for yours. Ma'am is acceptable."

Humiliation and emasculation ceded gradually and equally to distrust. Suspicion came next, and distaste, and animosity. His mind had been invaded - breached, somehow, in a transgression against that most fundamental human right of autonomy of thought.

"Perhaps, *Ma'am*, it would be best to continue our consultation another day."

"You are incorrect. There is no *perhaps*, only *is* and *is not*."

Ma'am's first voyage into the existential read like a corollary to the letter Every left for Alvin in a P.O. box; one of the morbid errands he'd run in the hours before his death.

"That similarity is not a coincidence, professor Alvin Bonman."

The hairs stood on Alvin's neck and the lightheadedness returned in full force. Assertiveness under those conditions was hard to come by, but Alvin decided to try.

"Why ask me questions you know the answers to? Why am I teaching geology to an encyclopedia with scales? You want to know what's on my mind - fucking read it yourself and let me relax in my cell for another five months."

"I am not reading your mind professor Alvin Bonman, and I mean no offense. The foundation of what you perceive to be a disagreement is rooted in our disparate evolved sociality, and I am willing to forsake my own if you are willing to accept. I mean to offer you an apology. Do you accept?"

Alvin had no doubt by this time that Ma'am knew full well his intentions to accept her apology. Still, he was human, after all, and the humility she'd shown in extending it was a compelling enough reason to stay in his plastic chair.

"Yes. But I would like to ask you another question now, if I may. And for the sake of this conversation, it is important that I am allowed to do the asking - whether you know what I will say or not. Okay?"

"That is acceptable."

"Good. I want to know about that disparity you mentioned, sociality, behavior, all of it - and I need to know how it informs your intimate knowledge of things you have no credible means of knowing."

"That is also acceptable. You must first know that although the result was mechanically different, our respective progression toward intelligence were governed by much the same network of pressures. Ours began, as is the tendency, with bacteria.

"The end of the Carboniferous period was brought about, in part, by a bacterial mutation that allowed for the consumption of fallen primordial trees. Before the mutation, no decay mechanism existed to free the carbon dioxide absorbed by those plants in life, and so the atmosphere was inundated with higher proportions of oxygen. It was also around this time that Pangea was forming."

"I am familiar with the Carboniferous period, Ma'am."

"Of course. Allow me, then, to inform you of the implications. It was among the Carboniferous swamps, having assurances that moisture was always somewhere within reach, that amphibians could afford to stray incrementally further from pools of water. Reptilian characteristics were favored for some, and, gradually, my ancestors and yours freed themselves entirely from the constraints of their aquatic habitats. When geology and bacteria succeeded in bringing about the end of the Carboniferous, oxygen and carbon dioxide levels stabilized and reptilians were unleashed upon a drier world. They found it well suited to them.

"Reptilians did not merely proliferate, they diversified. And what you call the Permian period, as you understand, professor Alvin Bonman, was not itself homogeneous in climate just because you have classified it as one unified era. Continental drift, celestial phenomena including no shortage of minor impacts, and volcanism -

particularly toward the end - contributed to a variable global biome tantamount to the Pleistocene in its demands for special adaptability."

Alvin leaned back in his seat, suddenly confident in the possibility that he remained the true expert in the room.

"You haven't told me much of anything I don't know, Ma'am. Adaptive radiation is a relatively basic premise of our understanding of the natural world. Filling an ecological niche at the right time and place does not explain what you're able to do."

"It unequivocally does, professor Alvin Bonman."

"I'm listening."

"You are listening, constantly and often without the conscious intention. Hearing is, in your view, the second most essential sense available to you. Would you agree?"

"Sounds about right."

"And the first?"

"Sight, obviously."

"And the least?"

"I could do without smell, I guess."

Alvin worried briefly, in plain view of her huge and dynamic set of nostrils, that he'd ventured too close to her elusive limit to polite discourse. Thankfully she gave no inclination of offense.

"Therein lies the primary physiological difference between your species and mine, professor Alvin Bonman. You speak of adaptive radiation skillfully, and, for a man specializing in the field of geology, I understand you have a functional knowledge of convergent evolution - if you forgive my saying so."

"Am I forgiving you for calling me a one trick pony or scanning my mind for Darwin's notes on finches?"

"Both are acceptable."

"Fine. Please, carry on."

"Both our species responded to similar pressures in, originally, similar ways. In yours, bipedal locomotion evolved in response to the insurmountable pressures of collecting sustenance from diminishing forest habitats. Walking upright allowed your predecessors to expand their foraging areas, and to avoid predation as they went by spotting nearby threats from above tall grass. My physiology was selected, naturally, to allow for long distance, low energy excursions between patches of vegetation during periods of drought."

"Sounds like we have more in common than it seems, Ma'am. So what was the big difference, exactly?"

"Fruit."

"Fruit?"

"Fruit, professor Alvin Bonman, evolved during the Cretaceous period as a symbiosis between plants and animals. Trees attracted foraging animals with their fruits' attractive colors and accessibility, animals consumed them, and some hours afterward the animal excreted seeds specially evolved to endure digestion. The animals became vessels of expansion in directions that wind alone could not be expected to carry a spore - with the added benefit of fertilizing the soil around the seed by the very nature of the process.

"In order to capitalize on so seemingly equitable an arrangement, animals - including your ancestors - required vision tuned to distinguish colorful fruit from a backdrop of green leaves. Your lineage has enjoyed the benefits since - canopy dwelling primates notwithstanding. My ancestors had no such pressure. When we ventured from place to place, we relied upon our sense of smell. And, having evolved into slow moving, cumbersome bipeds, only those of us who could smell a predator coming from a distance stood a chance of surviving its arrival."

"That is incredible, Ma'am. It stands to reason that your social behavior would diverge from ours when the sense we take most for granted is your go-to. I am impressed, I mean that, but it doesn't rectify the *glaring* problem. Plenty of species have evolved a heightened sense of smell. A few have evolved bipedalism. Why should I expect that arbitrary combination to give you insight into my thoughts and a perfect understanding of Martian geology?"

"Are you a nervous man, professor Alvin Bonman?"

"No."

"Surely you have known nervous men?"

"I believe you already know the answer to that."

"Professor Every Daniels was nervous, yes, and I will assure you now that the time will come when all your questions regarding your friend are answered. He is relevant to the present topic, professor Alvin Bonman, but not directly."

"He was nervous since childhood. Some people have that problem, some people don't. Every just happened to have it pretty bad. But, no, I'm not the type."

"I cannot fault you for regarding the trait as a problem, given the nature of your species and of the civilization you've built. I would ask you however, professor Alvin Bonman, to consider the evolutionary benefit in what I will refer to henceforth as a 'general apprehension'."

"I think its clear enough, Ma'am, that fear *is* one strategy among a large number that can help prey animals avoid predation. Keeps them on their toes, so to speak, and alive long enough to procreate. But I would argue that there are better strategies."

"It is true that banal fear formed the premise for general apprehension. But like your stone tools and your fire, it was an evolutionary path that, in conjunction with the necessary physiology, left great room for refinement. Your hominid graduation to sentience occurred as both result and requirement of applying intelligence toward the manipulation of resources, an informational feed-back loop between your environment and your fingertips. Ours, of course, was vastly different.

"As we walked the dust and dunes and open expanses of our time, our proverbial ears attuned incessantly to the distant hiss of gorgonopsids, consciousness became an inevitability. Those among us who sensed the furthest, who could conceive of space and direction relative to ourselves, who could imagine the course the predator would take and adjust our own accordingly; those were the survivors, the predecessors, the fathers. It was his general apprehension for everything sharing his environment that linked him so inextricably to it. But it was a much more fundamental, purely physical trait that predisposed us to our destiny as a species free from the scarcity of information that plagues yours now. Do you know which trait that was, professor Alvin Bonman?"

"Well it certainly wasn't your eyes."

"Nor was it our sense of humor."

Perhaps she had one after all.

"I'm listening, Ma'am. But I'll tell you, since you've already read my diary anyway, that I'm not the sort of man who will believe it just because you've said it."

"That is acceptable for the time being. It is our olfactory bulb, professor Alvin Bonman, the region of our brain corresponding to the sense of smell. You will recall that you were unsettled just minutes ago by the realization that my nostrils are the dominant feature on my face. That is also acceptable. There exists in nature no parallel to this organ outside of the most highly developed eyes, and even those are blind by comparison."

"They are impressive. I noticed, admittedly, that they're stereoscopic, and can contract or expand like my pupils. I can't say I've met a bloodhound with that kind of toolkit."

"It would be disingenuous to equate their contractions and expansions to the involuntary adjustments your eyes make in the presence or absence of light. It is a conscious process, directional, deliberate, and the mechanism for our success."

There was the indignation. Alvin was sure of it now.

"How is that?"

"Very recently, a theory that you are not familiar with has been developed regarding the long distance migration of various bird species. It is an accepted human belief that their ability to navigate is predicated upon detecting the Earth's magnetic field. The new theory asserts that quantumly entangled electrons within the animal's eye are excited by light, that the magnetic field exerts a directional influence upon their spin, and that the molecules to which they belong are principally affected. Activated by reactions with the altered chemical, other chemicals are released in the eye that form visual representations of the magnetism responsible. This is valid.

"Some biologists have postulated, likewise, that a lock and key explanation for the sense of smell among numerous species, yours included, is insufficient to account for the stupendous variety of molecules an individual can distinguish by scent. Some, albeit too few, have considered the likelihood that only a mechanism capable of reproducing an equally vast quantity of configurations could be responsible for the reception and categorization of those molecules. That mechanism is presently called quantum indeterminacy. This is valid."

Alvin was not an easy man to confuse, but Ma'am seemed to have made a mission of it.

"You are confused, professor Alvin Bonman. I ask that you believe me when I say that you will understand shortly."

"I'm not so sure I can."

"Might I explain the migratory birds again?"

"That won't be necessary, Ma'am. It's not that I don't understand what you're saying - which, to be fair, is partially true - it is that I am having a difficult time believing you. Increasingly."

"This is not acceptable, professor Bonman. It is vitally important that you make a concerted effort toward cooperating with me."

"I'm not a nervous man, Ma'am, but I am one with a healthy sense of skepticism and a high regard for his species. Ask those five out there," he gestured abruptly toward the divider, his first visible obstruction of protocol, "they'll vouch for us. Forgive me for being untoward, which should be easy given what you claim to expect from me, but there are seven billion of us, and there's one of you, and I learned in kindergarten which is better. You are something, *Ma'am*, maybe even someone. But you're not human, and you're sure as hell not the authority on what is or is not the reality of our own god damn planet."

"Are you upset?"

"No, Ma'am. I am honest."

"I would argue that honesty is much like the age of the earth. It depends to some degree on your perspective."

"And I would argue the opposite."

"Let us argue then, professor Alvin Bonman, so that you might see the perils in your relativistic truth."

"By all means. It's your playpen."

"You are a man of science. Science, for centuries, has been your species' best answer to the shortcomings of your physiology; a prosthetic extension you affix as compensation for the cumulative dilution of your senses. It, as a consequence, has served as the crutch for which the stunting of your natural development can be blamed."

"It was sure as hell good enough to raise you back from the dead, wasn't it?"

"It certainly was."

Ma'am's eyelids twitched. Alvin hadn't known she'd had them. Her nostrils were narrowed then to a diameter below what he could detect with his eyes, and Alvin considered whether it had been premature to believe she was beyond offending. She spoke again in her synthetic way, and Alvin feared there was more to hear than indignation.

"You've learned that my presence here is the result of your own species' efforts and technological ingenuity. But it required days before you could venture a guess toward professor Every Daniels' meaning, isn't that true? A moth, a proof of concept, coincidence, what of them? You spent days reading the words he left behind for you; your nights racked with rumination, all your nervous energy dedicated to falsifying his claim that your species rocked with blissful ignorance on the precipice of extinction - supported all the while by his long record of mental diagnoses.

"Gradually you put the pieces together, as keen professor Every Daniels expected you would. And still, bogged by the inflexible film of skepticism demanded by your science, it was not until very recently, during the course of this conversation, in fact, that you have allowed yourself to finally consider what is true."

Alvin finished his water. His mouth was dry when he spoke.

"What's that?"

"That your extinction is imminent, as my extinction had been imminent, and your species brought me back to prevent it."

"Bullshit."

"I hope that you will allow me to finish my explanation, professor Alvin Bonman. To do otherwise would be to bet your species on bullshit."

Alvin shrugged unconvincingly.

"Not like I have anywhere else to be."

"That answer is acceptable. Might I explain the migratory birds again?"

"Absolutely not."

"Very well. Shall I explain the mechanism for our success, then?"

"You can try."

"That is acceptable, although I understand that you have already begun to approach the conclusion yourself, professor Alvin Bonman. Whether you are critical of your own assessment is beside the point."

"I wouldn't mind if you sped up the process."

"Not unlike aviary navigation and the broader process of complex olfaction, our senses benefitted from the inclusion of mechanisms at the quantum level. Your term for this will become 'Quantum Nuance'."

"*Will become?*"

"Precisely."

Alvin sat up straight in his chair.

"You see professor Alvin Bonman, our graduation toward sentience was subject to such ecological pressures that survival could not be achieved without senses transcending the immediate."

"And even then it wasn't enough."

"A harsh truth, and still another matter subject to perspective. Extinction is a permanent state, as you know, professor Alvin Bonman, and yet here I sit."

"A little wishful thinking never hurt I guess. Perhaps semantics take some of the sting off too. I wouldn't know, my species is doing perfectly well."

"You'll recall what I said earlier about the word *perhaps*. You'll remember my claim that there are only *is* and *is nots*. You haven't forgotten professor Every Daniels' impressive interpretation on the fallaciousness of coincidence, and so too will you remember his charmingly misguided foresight in coining the *Statisticians* for the name of my kind.

"In any case, professor Alvin Bonman, it is the misfortune of your species that, although you can recall a great many things, you cannot *precall*. That is the preliminary difference between you and I as we sit across this table, arguing the semantics of semantics."

"Wait - Ma'am, maybe I am confused. You mean to tell me that your sage, all knowing species could see the future, could 'precall' and - correct me if I'm wrong - still went fucking *extinct*? I think I'll hold onto my hands and my scientific method if that's the alternative, thank you."

"In your sarcastic hostility, professor Alvin Bonman, there is a grain of factual importance. By virtue of the ability of our olfactory bulbs," she tapped a slight bulge in the flesh between her eyes, "we can detect, categorize, and anticipate the course of any sequence of events within a relative space. All things in this space - itself established by the magnetic field of our sun - depend on what your species, in your naivety, refer to as quantum indeterminacy.

"Doubtless a consequence of your fundamental desire for well balanced equations, you perceive quantum information as the unknowable point on a curve of probabilities which, by virtue of your having observed it, is catalyzed into existence. This is invalid. It is your lack of understanding, and your egotistical willingness to operationalize your attention, that have resulted in this misunderstanding."

"I'm still waiting for that grain."

"My olfactory bulb is designed to process quantum nuance, and my nose to physically track the spacial sequence. Like flocks in the hue of a vibrant blue magnetic field - I sense the past, the present, and the preselected future. I need only look.

"The rest of my body, as you can plainly see, is designed for continual migration and uprooting plants from the dirt. We anticipated the Great Dying long enough in advance to fear it as a matter of culture, and not nearly long enough to selectively mate for opposable thumbs. We could not escape the fate of our species, professor Alvin Bonman, because we didn't have the hands for it. The best we could do was wait for yours."

Someone tapped on the glass. It was Brady - his wrist against the divider, a watch with blurry hands no doubt approaching seven o'clock, conventional time.

"Before you go, professor Alvin Bonman, remind me - do you know how your species discovered us? How the process of reviving me began?"

"Every hinted at it, and some of the geologists in my dormitory got to see the holes before they changed protocol. There was a lot of speculation about what it all meant, and I can definitely say that nobody else was in the parking lot outside the fucking ball park. But I do remember the gist, and I had a lot of time to work through the hypotheticals during the last five months."

"I understand that you have reservations."

"A few."

"Please make them known. There is no sense in keeping secrets now."

"Couldn't agree more. Can you explain to me how a species with four cumbersome digits per stump etched mechanically perfect carvings in mechanically perfect intervals around two craters in the earth?"

"This posed no physiological challenge. We anticipated rainfall - time, amount, and acidity. Etching our messages into the limestone was only a matter of redirecting the water through channels, simple enough for a chimpanzee to dig, and allowing time and erosion to serve as pen and ink."

"How did you dig the holes?"

"It was not our burden to dig the holes. Opportunity will always present itself on so great a temporal scale. Ask your most important question, won't you? You intend to discredit me in the details, but you will not succeed in it."

"Why were there only males in the grave? Are you not a female?"

"I am. That is a keen question, and you would find great interest in hearing it answered, but now is not the time and that is not the question."

"So be it. You deny that your kind are 'Statisticians', but you should be qualified to answer this one, I think. It's a little bit of a soft ball. Tell me - what are the odds that in any given one-thousand year period, one slate of geologic time *among ten million*, a species will advance technologically to the point of reviving an extinct species of moth, stumble upon the opportunity to do the same for a lost Paleozoic intelligence, and, *coincidentally*, go extinct themselves? Seems to me, Ma'am, that there are two explanation, none less shitty than the other."

"I would like to hear your explanations."

"Explanation one. You've manipulated us into reviving your species - basically forced our hand by leading us toward evidence of an extinction that ain't gonna fucking happen."

"And explanation two?"

"Statistics say the same god damn thing that Every did, and nobody listened. The other option is that we bought the ticket to our own extinction the moment we brought you back, and you'll be waiting at the door to tear it yourself. You'll kill us all, everything, clean slate. Then you'll bring your people back."

"What if I could prove that either scenario is wrong before you lay in your bed tonight? I ask you - would you trust me then? Would you, a man with a mind shaped for cooperation and hands fit for building - would you escape the fate of those species destined to live and die with neither?"

"I probably wouldn't believe you."

"Proof, professor Alvin Bonman, does not depend, to any degree, on your perspective."

"You sound like a scientist. Make your point."

"Survival, necessarily, takes many forms. Science has its place."

"I'd prefer proof over flattery, if you don't mind, Ma'am."

"In eighty-nine seconds it will be seven o'clock and the door will open. You will tell Brady Elway Thomas that I wish to speak with him. He will refuse. You will insist. A short time later, important looking men will bring you into an important looking room. Together you will contact the overnight team responsible for monitoring the Parker Solar Probe at The Johns Hopkins University Applied Physics Laboratory. You will direct their attentions to the Wide Field Imager presently directed toward the sun's corona, you will ask them to count to fifteen, and then you will have your proof."

The door handle began to rattle.

"I have more questions."

"You have time for one."

"Your physiology didn't account for the fact that you know what I mean to say before I've had the chance to say it. How can you know what I'm thinking?"

"We will look back on this conversation many times, professor Alvin Bonman, and we will discuss your thoughts in great detail. I, for one, am looking forward to it."

INSTALLMENT FIVE

It had been a long migration - their longest since Point-56792, or so went the chatter amongst the backwards-casters. Point-74709 had spent most of his own carrier phase gawking across the same bygone temporal plane. It was that matter, above all others, that he'd place an emphasis on correcting during his forty-year director phase allotment.

"We are here. The greatest densities of moisture retardant boughs are a two-nineteenths north-western horizon march. Former-half carrier phaselets depart at present to begin material collection, hastily and without spears. The last gorgonopsid with territory at this latitude and all its descendants have long since been forced south. Latter-half phaselets will be allowed to graze on the sphenophyta thickets one-twenty fifth horizon due west for a period of one-half day."

Even for a community armed with near omniscience and over one-hundred-thousand generations of experience, it had been an arduous migration for them all.

"At that time, latter-half phaselets shall rest in preparation for sunset fertilization. Former-half phaselets shall graze to that point and no later, as rainfall will be sparse beyond replenishing until mid-season."

"Yes Point-74709."

The physically smaller half of P-709's harem pressed on, exhausted and spearless, undaunted, indifferent. Most of the more developed females obliged their director's orders as well, the spines of their vestigial sails clung to backs dressed in sun dried scales.

P-709 watched them go with what little vision he'd inherited. To make observations in the crude way of senseless beasts was his hobby - or the nearest thing to it in his time and place and among his kind. Between the splotches and blurs, he saw enough of the spines on his departing harem to detect a resemblance to the hollow fangs of viper species two-hundred million years from twinkling in the eye of evolution.

"Point-74709?"

One of the fifty latter-half phaselets lingered behind.

"Hello, Point-74710. I am pleased by your visit, but regret your sacrifice in prime vegetation."

P-710's neck was too thick to turn more than thirty-five degrees. Instead she spun from her director, tracing the path of her fellow phaselets by gradually reorienting two constricted nostrils. Her point of observation bypassed them shortly thereafter, illuminating their forthcoming route in preemptive and absolute detail.

"You understand that precalling direct actions of our community and it's members is unauthorized at present, do you not, P-710?"

She carried on precalling.

"I do, P-709, and I also understand that it is equally unauthorized across phases and roles. It would be hard to argue that precalling my grazing misfortunes was anything but direct."

"You'll develop the same respect for flexibility as I have in your next phase, P-710."

"I am aware of that."

"So you have been working on your forward-casting, then? It is not enough to directly participate or backward-cast into communal discussions regarding events nearer the temporal horizon. It must be mastered on an individual level."

"I have, P-709."

"How far forward?"

"The mid Cretaceous."

"Impressive, P-710, especially for a carrier phaselet."

Nature saw to it that P-710's species evolved an extremely simplistic social structure. It was largely understood, most of all following the precalled discovery of their far-off Cenozoic parallels, that injecting any unnatural complexity into the intraspecies dynamic would only serve to generate friction.

Still, with sensory organs built like stereoscopic metal detectors sifting grains of probability for the telltale blip of certainty; with olfactory bulbs comprised of interwoven quantum processors and with minds designed for storage; their unified effort to peer a quarter-billion years into the future ensured that cultural pollination was inevitable.

One thing P-710's species inherited from humans, whether they'd intended it or not, was pride.

"It is the furthest an individual carrier phaselet has precalled by 49.853 million years, P-709. I recall that your most distant cast did not surpass the late Triassic."

P-709 had also put some emphasis on subduing his own sense pride as director.

"This is valid. I appreciate your commitment, P-710. Those efforts will prove invaluable when you enter your director phase. Precollection capacity generally septuples upon transitioning from the carrier phase. To increase by a factor of five may seem a tremendous leap, but you'll recall that, until Point-00131, the furthest an individual carrier phaselet had succeeded in precalling was forty revolutions. A two-hundred-year-maximum-precollection range was hardly enough forewarning to prevent our extinction."

"Much has changed since then, P-709."

"This is valid. It is also valid to say that much more will change, P-710, to a degree of uncertainty through which no individual or community can precall."

P-710 abandoned her observations of the grazing party when they physically reached the densest patches of sphenophyta. Her nostrils relaxed before her director, widening three-fold. It was one of the few social cues her species partook in - a signal of disarmament, visible even to their diminutive eyes. Once selection became a matter of choice rather than of nature, some eyesight had been retained to allow for sociality independent of quantum-nuance-based information gathering. Such a practice was viewed as too invasive between individuals, most having some small sense, at least, of a private self.

"We are all familiar with the Abrupt Post Human Interference Boundary, P-709. Our failure to reliably precall beyond it has been known since Point-55709, and attributed to a lack of effort since Point-71200. It is an entropic boundary - a higher plane of perceived variability - to be conquered with greater attention and superior effort, just as all boundaries before it were conquered. To that point, I believed that all, including yourself, were in agreement."

P-709 collected a spear from the top of a pile left behind when the two halves of his harem parted ways. P-710 considered precalling just far enough to gauge whether her director had the unprecedented intention to commit violence upon her, but dismissed the thought upon remembering her many brief, unauthorized forays into proud moments of her own future in that role.

"Tell me, P-710, when you've precalled your directorate - your hardships, your achievements, your migrations and your sunset fertilizations - what were their nature?"

"P-709, I - of course I practiced restraint in this, as all director bound carrier phaselets are expected to. I cannot comment on my own allotment, as, in deference to my future harem, hatched and unhatched, I have paid it no visit outside those glimpses required for climate assessments and migratory planning."

In observing the humans, her species had also learned to lie.

"Most of all I have avoided, as per custom across all directorates, precalling any and every fertilization to which I will be party. I respect the modesty of every carrier phaselet, as I have expected every past director to respect mine."

A grain of truth was often helpful when one intended to imbue some prospect of legitimacy into their chosen deceit. P-710 had employed that trick of the trade rather tactfully, or so she believed.

"This season will be my last as director, P-709. I will be buried alongside my lineage, and yours, and you will oversee it, and so too will you be buried alongside me. I do not have the time or the will to punish you for your curiosity, nor do I hold you in lower esteem for your pride. I prefer to spend the last days over which I hold sway - these fleeting moments still mine for breathing and for standing and speaking at the summit of our grave - productively."

Twin gifts forged in the misbehavings of Earth's great tectonic plates, P-710 peaked over the lip of the nearer of two massive gouges in the planet's crust. It had been deeper, once.

"In one season my days will be measured in decay. In one billion seasons my contribution will be told by the strength of a foundation built of my bones. I do not blame you for your passing glances into an exciting time in your life. I have taken many such glances. There is another matter much more deserving of the breath I still have sway over."

"You will be remembered fondly across my allotment, P-709, and every other allotment I have felt compelled to observe."

P-709 paid no mind to his successor's hybrid of pandering and apology, be her assurances genuine or improvised compliments strung together for his benefit. He had already begun to scribble in the dust with the sharp end of the spear, no simple thing for a cumbersome biped with claws evolved for gouging roots and hands still shaped for bearing weight.

Emboldened after their exchange regarding the unauthorized practice, P-710 precalled the borderline unintelligible end result of P-709's scrawling. She refrained, as a matter of instinct, from sparing him the remaining effort by admitting she'd already observed its culmination. Where precalling events relating to the direct actions of the living was unauthorized, attempting to influence their behavior in advance of its fulfillment was inconceivable. Those who had attempted it, according to the murmurs of backward-casting carrier phaselets, inevitably lost their ability to precall at precisely the moment such a consideration struck. It was a temporary affliction, but an invariable one.

"Do you know what these are, P-710?"

P-710 believed she knew.

"Parallel rows of points, line-segments, triangles, and squares divided into two clusters."

"I'll ask, P-710, that you place more emphasis on understanding the subtle during your forward-casting exercises to come. To know the nature of a distant moment only at its broadest level is no better than to know tomorrow in absolute detail."

Her nostrils halved in sized. Insofar as a member of her species was able, P-710 took it personally.

"For now, I shall explain it to you, P-710. Each cluster represents a small portion of the genetic sequence responsible for governing the manufacturing process of a specific biological trait. One of them is present in our cells, the other found in various forms throughout a small number of pure reptiles - alive, extinct, and yet to evolve. I would ask that you decide which is which now. Is this acceptable?"

"Yes, Point-74709."

Outside of greetings, reverting to an individual's formal name to express displeasure was a behavior borrowed from human parents of the 19th, 20th, and early 21st centuries. It was an act of defiance - and a small one, given that P-710 set to work immediately thereafter dissecting the nuanced structure of her own anatomy.

"The second cluster is present in us both. You've included the minimum number of nucleotide pairs from the beginning of the gene to allow for differentiation from any other genetic sequence."

"This is valid. What is the gene responsible for?"

"Sequential hermaphroditism."

"Explain what it is and why it was necessary."

P-710 did not need to precall to anticipate the question.

"It is an adaptation with origins in our quadrupedal ancestors. During times of intense climactic variability, sexual dimorphism resulted in a resource disparity between the sexes of our species. Males, generally twice the size of females by mass during that period, required prohibitive amounts of food and water. Only males with relatively low levels of testosterone remained at a size practical for surviving in periods of drought."

"That is only half the story, P-710."

A moment of intense focus, a sharp breath of validation.

"Sexual dimorphism was reigned in during that period, but far from selected out completely. Climactic fluctuations had become so dependable - counterintuitive as such a statement may be - that survival depended upon a dynamic biological response. Ancestral populations dense in males grazed themselves into localized extinction. Populations devoid of males were unable to breed. It was a small mutation in a single hereditary lineage, from a single generation, that bridged that gap."

"Explain it to me."

"The mechanism for testosterone inhibition already existed by that time, responsible for reducing the size of males while preserving the species' ability to reproduce. To capitalize more effectively on that existing mechanism, all that was required was a genetic trigger."

"This is valid. You may elaborate."

"Embryonic development begins across species in the default female state - unhatched males being dependent on the introduction of testosterone to physiologically diverge. The crucial mutation was to suppress the release of testosterone in all hatchlings to protect from the over-extension of resources requisite to males. Only during periods of abundance - be it one season during a single revolution, or a period of heavy rainfall amidst a decade of drought - would the females best predisposed to capitalize on that abundance overcome the activation threshold for the otherwise dormant embryonic testosterone producing gland. Resource availability permits the transition from female to male. Resource acquisition determines which individuals will achieve it."

"Why then, P-710, do we only have one male to occupy the director phase even during periods of consistent abundance?"

P-710 was excited to answer her director's next question, and, abruptly, dismayed to find that she could not.

Another psychological stowaway from their excursions into a later time, and perhaps the most potent, was embarrassment. Although sociality was not as intrinsic to their ascent toward intelligence as the humans, P-710's ancestors had necessarily begun as, and habitually remained, herd animals. There was much to gain from cooperation, and, insofar as they intended to preserve it, some individual pressures toward humility.

Modesty, too, had been among the consequences of that divergence in standards of association. It was precisely the reason that any precollection of fertilizations was regarded with such disgust. An individual suspected of precalling so much as the goings-on of a future harem around the chasms, a place they visited only during the brief fertilization period, would be subject to decades of shame and unkindness. P-710 had been true to her word - never venturing close enough to the fertilization site to justify such treatment. But there were many causes for shame, and embarrassment, and in the presence of a director universally held in high esteem, P-710 felt them now.

"I do not know, P-709."

"Can you tell me, at least, when the single directorate came to be?"

This one, at least, she knew.

"Point-00000, of course."

"Do you recall why we take these names? Why you are Point-74710? Why your predecessor, grazing at this very moment with her own predecessors, is called Point-74711?"

"Our director phase names represent the moment of our respective allotments, expressed in decimals which describe the passage of time between our species' graduation to sentience and the Permian-Triassic extinction event."

"Correct. Our success, P-710, when measured in terms of special longevity, can be attributed to that knowledge made accessible to us by the pressures of ancestral hardship. We have the capacity, together, to assess the past and ascertain those things which are inevitable. But you, perhaps the best equipped of all to precall distant events, could not, moments ago, describe even the nature of your genes, and still cannot describe the principal construct of our society and the position you are one season from assuming."

P-710 was upset, and famished, enough of either to strongly consider departing while there was time left to scavenge for decent thickets.

"P-710, I hope that you will understand my harshness for the lesson that it is. To suppress the phase transition from female to male, by restricting resource access regardless of abundance, was a deliberate effort made and agreed upon. First to consider is our individual longevity. Our bodies, in their first phase, regenerate almost indefinitely in preparation for the eventual transition. Cells begin to degrade at a higher rate in the second phase. Despite all the efforts made to preserve them, male cells will cease regenerating after forty years - an allotment of time nature deemed sufficient for genetic propagation.

"Second, and understandably more difficult to grasp for any individual, is this. Beginning with P-000, a lineage was established - a temporal hierarchy and chain of custody for the preservation and expansion of knowledge. You alone, nor I, have the capacity to adequately precall all the events to which our species will one day be subject. That requires a species wide effort. Every member must commit centuries to the furtherance of our kind in the role of carrier. It is only by that individual progression, from adolescent former-half carrier phaselets to your own fertile latter-half, are we fit to appreciate the importance of our ultimate role as director."

P-710 did not yet understand her predecessor's harshness for the lesson it was, despite his efforts, but his words had at least abated some of her agitation.

"P-709?"

"Yes, P-710?"

"I have been attempting to identify the first genetic sequence, but can find no direct parallel."

"Yes. There are, on occasion, no direct parallels to find. It is those such occasions which most challenge us. They are our present hardships, our modern pressures, the narrow slits through which we cannot pass until we've reimagined our shape. If we can do it, we emerge refined. If we cannot, we stagnate behind a boundary we have forced ourselves to regard as impregnable. Time and space are more than just the hard parts, P-710."

P-710 got the message. She would be director in one season, but she was not director now. P-709 held that title still, and he meant to test her while he could.

"May I try again, P-709?"

"You must."

Minutes passed. With no decent point of reference, directional or temporal, P-710 cast her nostrils every which way - broadening them to filter vast swaths of data, narrowing them any time she brushed a potential solution. Upon recognizing the futility in re-canvasing the past, present, and future all on her own, she took a shortcut - a deliberate recall of one forward-casting exercise she and dozens of other latter-half carrier phaselets had participated in - the joint precollection of a distant time; a time decidedly inaccessible to her as an individual. For the sake of stoking at the embers of her comparatively unwieldy sense of self importance, this temporal detour was not at all the path of least resistance. For the sake of reaching a meaningful conclusion in a single lifetime - it was necessary, and it worked.

"Megalania. The largest monitor lizard species to have existed, endemic to Australia during the Pleistocene. Its status as longstanding apex predator can be attributed to its size, its venom, and, in no small part, to its dynamic reproductive strategy."

P-709's nostrils relaxed. He had refrained from precalling his successor's answer. He was glad for his restraint, and he was impressed.

"Which evolutionary strategy?"

"Protogenesis. Although sex remained its primary reproductive mechanism - vital for preserving genetic diversity - female megalania were capable, in times of mate scarcity, of sexless reproduction. The genetic sequence you asked me to identify is not identical, but sufficiently overlaps with the megalania gene to ascertain its basic function."

"How did you come upon this realization, P-710?"

"I had to reimagine the question, P-709. Rather than following a network of certainties, you challenged me to address the problem from a different perspective; to make those observations which are possible to make, and to draw those conclusions with which they are most in agreement."

P-710 was still brimming with pride and expectation when her predecessor turned away, spear in hand and praise un-given.

"Come, P-710. I have another thing to show you. I insist that you do not precall now, as you did minutes ago while I toiled in the dirt."

Embarrassment. Forced to walk her swaying walk - awkward and difficult, as if she and her species were punished for their eagerness to escape quadrupedalism with an eternal rash, she joined P-709 and titled her head to sense his latest drawing visually.

"Can you tell me what I've drawn, P-710?"

P-710 did not bother telling. Instead she lifted her tree trunk arm and flexed her rudimentary knuckle, pointing with great effort in the direction of the second enormous hole in the Earth. P-709 dropped his spear, dividing his crudely completed drawing of their ancestral nesting reservoir into two hemispheres.

"Yes. I would ask that you now explain its purpose during fertilization seasons of the distant past."

P-709 knew intuitively that such a request would cause some discomfort, and so decided to clear the air.

"Recollection of fertilization seasons is conditionally authorized, P-710. All participants of that fertilization period must be dead, and the object of your recollection may not be perverse. I can assure you that it is not."

Recollection was considerably easier to achieve than precollection. Even a former-half carrier phaselet could recall the earliest days of multicellular life all by herself. P-710 was considerably more capable than that, and, with her director's permission, made short work recalling what she needed to formulate her response.

"When Point-23678 and his harem first precalled the Great Dying, a mechanism to preserve our species in some meaningful way was conceived and implemented. One egg per fertilization season would be stored and buried in such a way that fossilization was inevitable. Sediments accumulated above the previous layer until the next level was sufficiently deep for its own ring. Should a technologically advanced and physiologically amenable post-Great-Dying species arise, the prevailing belief was that they would be compelled by curiosity to gather enough genetic detail from the multitude of embryos for special revival to occur."

"So why was the last egg buried during Point-55709's directorate?"

"Precollection extended to the Abrupt Post Human Interference Boundary, corresponding to the human year 2017. Human technology had advanced sufficiently, at least, to allow for practical genetic parsing. Unfortunately, it resulted in our discovering that to preserve genetic material for the duration was outside the scope of our own. There will be no template of our species available for the humans to follow."

"Have you considered how that problem may be addressed, P-710? Have you any intention, while the directorate is yours to guide, of solving our species' great conundrum?"

"Of course, P-709. I will preserve and extend the diligent works of our predecessors. With enough momentum of effort, the Abrupt Post Human Interference Boundary will be shattered. Behind it, we will find our true course to survival."

P-710 was proud to reassert the enduring cause of her species. P-709 was displeased to hear it.

"I hope that you will understand my harshness for the lesson that it is."

Embarrassment, shame, familiar apprehension.

"Is that not my role as director, P-709? To push the boundaries of our knowledge?"

"You are attempting to push an immovable boundary, P-710, when all you need to do is find your way through the slits."

"How?"

P-709 handed the carrier phaselet his spear.

"Precisely as you did before. Reason, observe, conclude. The humans have a word for that process. Do you know it?"

That process was familiar to her, vaguely, but the word her director associated it with became much more elusive a thing. Definitions were precisely the sort of concrete data her kind could collect from the distant future with the ease of siphoning water through porous eggshell. It was human abstraction that demanded effort; at least, it seemed, for anyone who was not P-709.

"I know it, in a way, P-709. But I do not know the word."

"Science."

P-710 was puzzled, evidenced by the aimless darting of her nostril holes.

"P-709 - their science, as we've come to know it, is not so broadly defined and... slippery. It is a meticulous process characterized by standards and governed by certainties. Simply put - science is the human invention meant to analog our own physiological mechanism for deduction."

"If achieving a certainty requires nuanced observation, P-710, how could the humans know where to start?"

"From the beginning, presumably."

"It is in your nature and mine to know the beginning precisely as it was, P-710, but not in the humans'. It is human nature to puzzle over the beginning, and the surrounding, and the impending. They will puzzle for centuries, millions of minds, puzzling all the time, whispering of puzzles to the children who will carry on puzzling when they've died content without answers."

"How could a species with such simple minds ever come to dominate this world?"

P-710 was convinced with no nuanced observation to speak of that her director had taken some offense.

"You have placed yourself behind a boundary, P-710. Find the slit."

"Are you insinuating, Point-74709, that the humans' prosthetic mechanism for attaining knowledge is superior to our own?"

"In some ways they are indistinguishable. In others; yes, decidedly so."

P-710's face would have been red if it were human.

"As forthcoming director, I feel compelled to remind you that their species was nearly extinguished several times over a negligible period of revolutions. Their class of species inherited meaningful portions of our genes, and what benefit was it to them? For one-hundred and forty million revolutions they scurried fearfully from footprint to Archosauria footprint. It took another sixty-six million of nearly uncontested reign to develop imagination enough to spit berry ink on cave walls. They are evolutionary meanderers, the imbecilic winners of eons of relative climactic stability; their prize being opposable thumbs deprived of us by circumstance, their brains just complex enough to twiddle them."

"Excellent, P-710. It appears that we are in agreement."

"How can you misconstrue my meaning so completely? I believe the migration has taken a toll on you, P-709. I suggest you find sustenance so that you might be more sensible before the fertilization."

"I do not misconstrue, and I've fertilized on an emptier stomach. We are in agreement, Point-74710, because you have, in listing their shortcomings, described those qualities which most endow mankind with a proclivity for survival that we ourselves will not achieve. It is in the very act of surmounting their hardships that the humans prove, and likewise refine, their vastness of adaptability.

"As a species they represent a fortuitous contradiction - a quandary, from our perspective. How might billions of intellectually, physically, and culturally disparate individuals achieve anything of benefit to the collective? Why would a collective of such volume pander to the whims of the individual? By their individuality they amass boundless knowledge, the concrete and the arbitrary; knowledge with origins to be found in any of one-hundred billion epicenters. By their unification they defend, support, and propagate those epicenters. You yourself have demonstrated the capacity of their nature to radiate itself - you have embraced their pride, and you have applied it to your message and so made hostilities of your words to me. I am not upset, P-710, I am empathetic. I am empathetic because I have learned empathy, just as I first learned and then disavowed pride in my carrier phase, just as I have endeavored to learn enough of the humans and their prosthetic knowledge to do as they've done."

"To do what, P-709?"

"To be clever. To be clever enough to spare our species from the permanence of extinction."

"If not to see beyond the Post Human Interference Boundary, then what is your plan to spare us of it?"

With care, but not without firmness, P-709 pulled the spear from his successor's grip.

"There is an undisturbed patch of sphenophyta thickets one-fifty-fourth horizon march south-east. Eat, P-710. Go now so that you might be satiated when it is discussed between the sun and moon; between my harem and yours."

Point-74709 stood at the western boundary of the grave that would become his body, patient and naked, disheveled, regal as a director could aspire to be. He had aspired to it, once. And so it had become his outward nature, and now, inwardly, he aspired only to do justice to it.

It was there his harem found him. First came the former-half carrier phaselets; fed from the scraps of vegetation left behind by their elders who preceded them at pasture, and still they trundled without complaint save the grumbles of their stomachs. They placed the boughs of wood requested without explanation in the shadow of their director, destined to hold his position some centuries later and so respectful of it.

Then came the latter-half carrier phaselets. Each was well rested and better fed in preparation for her reproductive duty - P-710 among them despite her omission from fertilization as forthcoming director. As one unified harem they looked upon the current occupant of the directorate, fledgling a title as it was.

There he stood on his perch of earth beside the grave chasm. There he stood, he and his dwindling stature testing the force of the breeze, decayed and wobbling at the very precipice of a foregone conclusion. Still he looked strong. P-709 had been a special director, and his harem would remember him fondly, and future harems would recall him with awesome reverence.

More impressive than the director's endeavors against nature for the right to a parting address, perhaps, were the products of his endeavors during the hours he'd had to himself.

"I hope you've all had your fill. As I said before, the rains will be light this season, and our efforts, necessarily, will be heavy."

P-709 gestured at the ground beyond his mound with the spear ensnared between his clawed fingers, the tip dulled and dirty and frilled with severed roots after hours spent carving shallow gouges into the earth. It was not so dull that the harem could not identify where the director intended their attentions to go.

"I ask that you observe with your eyes. Refrain, if you may, from nuanced observation at this time and place."

P-709's harem obliged him, huddling closely together, moving as a pack to the boundaries of the large congruent circles he'd carved into the most pliable dirt. With only the accounts of biologically cannibalized eyes to depend upon, many carrier phaselets did not appreciate the true nature of the circles until the most keen among them made it known. P-710, feeling very much the pride of an insider, made such a contribution to the benefit of the latter-half phaselet beside her.

"The ring on the right is not formed by a solid boundary. If you were to rest upon the ground and draw your eye near to it, you would see that it is a genetic sequence."

"And on the left?"

P-710's eyes were no more capable than the carrier-phaselet who had posed the question - or any other member of her species, for that matter. Neither had P-709 given her any meaningful foundation during their conversation from which to draw a conclusion. Any answer she gave without cheating, thus, would be pure conjecture. Thankfully, P-709 spoke again before she need offer any.

"For many generations we have gathered around these two great tears in the world; twin representations of the destructive capacity of nature, and, at once, our chosen incubator for those generations which will blossom from our footprints. They have also housed, at various times, our sincerest efforts toward propagating this species long after our bones and the bones of our offspring become the dusts which line the first cavity. The second cavity has become a testament to our failure - one forsaken egg per season the sum of its bricks; our mislead sacrifices the sum of its mortar.

"Many directors have come and gone since last we contributed to that well of disappointment. Yet here we stand. Why do we return to this place? Is it instinct? Surely it is instinct to preserve our predecessors' modesty by refusing to precall their transgressions here - but what will those transgressions be? Before you, carved into the sediment crust of this sacred place, are my own representations. These circles, if you should be so humble as to rest upon the ground and know them, represent, as my parting word and eternal legacy as director, the future of our transgressions, and of our species, and of the world."

The carrier-phaselet, compelled first by the forthcoming director and thereafter by the incumbent, was first to step forward. She was first to press herself against the dirt to inspect the border of the circle on the left, first to see the celestial scenes laid out in their dozens to establish a ring. She was joined in short order by the rest, all on the ground appreciating their director's craftsmanship, all puzzling over the meaning. All but P-710; she herself remained standing so her voice might carry across each humbled ear along its path to the director they would go soon without.

"You mean for us to dedicate the daylight hours of fertilization seasons to come carving these markings into the craters?"

"This is valid, P-710."

"Why have you chosen to withhold this announcement until your parting season?"

It was an accusation. Pairs of nostrils swung by their dozens toward the next director, though every eye remained steadfastly downward in obedient, sacred, solidarity. The current director gave his answer with a mind for reinforcing that nature so uniquely his which first begot their regard for him.

"Yes, P-710. It seemed only right to dedicate as many seasons as were mine to careful and meticulous reflection on a matter to which yours and all subsequent directorates will be subject."

One foot on either side of that directorate, P-710 had long since begun to seek and savor the wafting essences of her approaching power; the consequence being an indignation as of yet unconsecrated by a moment's experience.

"What is this matter you have unilaterally chosen to impose upon my directorate, P-709? Did I have no right to a consultation?"

"You had your consultation, P-710."

P-709 descended his earthen pulpit. On level ground he approached his successor, and she her unexpected adversary. They met nose to nose on the virgin dirt that divided the future he'd scrawled, surrounded by the harem which would soon be hers to lead.

"I hope you will understand my harshness for the lesson that it is."

P-709 set the pitch and tone of the exchange there and then; ensuring that any words they shared would be sufficiently loud to be heard without effort by all the harem.

"I do not need your lessons, P-709. In precollection, I have surpassed you in the carrier phase and will surpass you in the director phase. This is the measure of a director. My lessons will be sought. Yours will be regarded as agitations; they will be remembered for their meandering, and so too for their harshness, but only for the baselessness of it, and then only as a cautionary tale to forthcoming directors."

For P-710's species, utter silence was the loudest gossip.

"P-710, your interpretations are your own -", this was far from an objective truth insofar as his audience was concerned, and at worst it was blasphemous, "- but it is my sincerest hope that you have retained enough esteem for the directorate to oblige me now. Will you hear what I have to say, be it curt or obscene or complimentary, and respond only when I have finished?"

It was a scathing insult spoken graciously. P-710 could do nothing but accept the humiliation and surrender without condition.

"Yes."

A small concession, P-709 finally lowered his voice.

"Thank you, P-710. Please stand here, with me, so that my harem may know that the sanctity of the position remains unperturbed, and that your harem may never recall that the standards for its acquiescence appeared so nearly compromised."

P-709 had extended her an olive branch, however frankly, and P-710, by abstention, had accepted it. The predecessor spoke then loudly enough to be heard above the successor's silent brooding.

"For millions of revolutions, I can say resolutely that the gravest hurdle to our longevity as a species, and so our vibrancy as living individuals, has been the impending extinction, and our inability to foresee a mechanism with both facility and inclination enough to reverse it. If there is disagreement to that point, I ask, with assurances of no ulterior motive, to speak yours openly and clearly."

No disagreement to speak of.

"To that point, then, we are all in agreement. It is to the resultant points that my perspective will diverge from yours, for now, and from the epochal precedent. In my view, it is not in the temporal distance or the entropy that we will find the root of our failure to observe beyond the Post Human Interference Boundary. Nor from this vantage can I conceive of our unveiling the solution to that conundrum of permanent extinction by virtue of redoubled efforts in precollection, Interference Boundary or no Interference Boundary. Where we have not precalled the sacred seasons our descendants will spend here in respect to their modesty - we have precalled scenes of their migrations, and their directors, and even the waning moments our last generation will spend knowing that demise had come at last for them. Why then, among one billion conversations, have we heard no mention of the human year 2019? Of their next great war? Of their colonization of the solar system? We have not heard it, because we will not know it."

The silence persisted, equal in breadth and still somehow more solemn. P-710 was sure to confine evidence of her befuddlement to the spaces between receptors in her mind - the signals they traded currently off-limits to wandering observations by director decree.

Why 2019? Why the added year?

"Allow me to remind you of my first two points so that you might persuade yourself to endorse them as valid. First, no strength of effort will result in our species detecting any information originating beyond the Post Human Interference Boundary. Second, it is disingenuous to assume that insights gained from beyond the Boundary will ensure the revival of our species on the part of mankind. Now that we have endured the punishment of honesty in assessing ourselves and our conundrum, we may begin to approach the problem in a manner more conducive to its rectification. P-710?"

"Yes, Point-74709?"

"Disclose to your future harem the nature of those genes you and I discussed early this day."

Narrated as he went by her summary of those genes for sequential hermaphroditism and protogenesis, P-709 moved on a limp toward the boundary of the circle on her left. By the time she had finished, he'd dragged his spear across its diameter; one circle thus divided into two hemispheres. For good measure, P-709 etched his own likeness into the northern half, and, in the southern, a shape that context persuaded P-710 to identify as a predatory lizard.

"Now please assess the purpose of the second ring, P-710. You are free to use any sense at your disposal, so long as your observations are restricted to the present."

"You have drawn a series of eighty-nine scenes crudely representative of the night sky from this location at various times throughout Earth history. Five, roughly corresponding in time to the planet's mass extinctions, have been defaced in proportion to the rate of species diversity loss. Forty-six depict dates beyond the Post Human Interference Boundary, presumably extrapolated from communal knowledge regarding the known trajectories of celestial bodies."

A gesture of gratitude among members of the species, P-709 tapped his successor gently on the shoulder. Reservedly flattered, P-710 responded as was customary - turning her body to expose her back and its sail. Growing at an accelerated rate since influxes of testosterone began to alter her physiology early the previous season - P-710's sail was the most substantial of all carrier phaselets. Her director completed the gesture by unfurling her sail with his clawed fingers - careful all the while not to puncture the sensitive membrane - so that the harem might gawk in appreciation of her status.

Another olive branch. Appeasement. P-710 could not decide whether to appreciate his courtesy or begrudge him for his tact; that is not to say she had no preference.

"This is valid, P-710. Now. Having considered our own shortcomings openly and shamelessly, we are free at last to assess our resources with sincerity, and our options with pragmatism. In making such assessments on my own, I can conclude, and humbly request that you concede, these three major tenets. The first is that our only hope for a temporary extinction lay in establishing a permanent, amicable, and more-or-less subsidiary relationship with the human race. May this relationship henceforth be regarded as an interspecies symbiosis."

Chatter among those carrier phaselets who had long since accepted their director's first tenet as a matter of universally agreed necessity; silence among those who had repurposed the pride they'd learned from human precollection into a brand of species nationalism.

"Second. In order to establish our symbiosis, we must make accessible our genetic composition in such a way that assures us, in accordance with our precollection of their most modern generation, will be technologically amenable. The inclusion of a mechanism for protogenesis will ensure that our survival thereafter will not be monopolized by technological availability, nor by human discretion. Further, should we hope to influence human receptivity to our greeting across time, we must appeal to their nature. Intrinsically, blatant evidence of a primordial intelligence will generate sensational curiosity among the humans. Equally, it will beget fear, hesitation, panic, and distrust. My third tenet addresses that response, and how we might circumvent it, and then, crucially, the Post Human Interference Boundary itself."

P-709 limped to his second circle in the dirt, visibly exhausted and endearingly resolved. His predecessor waited alone for the next tenet, the next instruction, the next declaration of a lame-duck director to which she and everyone were expected to be beholden. All the while, with mounting jealousy and frothing suspicion, she puzzled over his passing mention of the human year 2019.

"Third. I have come to a unique conclusion, and only through unique means which you may, at first, regard with some affront. I must remind you, tenderly, that all I have done, and how I have approached the business of doing it, was and will forever be in the interest of our species' future. The conclusion is this."

Of the eighty-nine he'd scribbled in the dirt, P-709 found the shortest route to one in particular. Broad and flat and well suited to his task, two swings of the foot were all he needed to upheave the milky way; to erase it from his timeline.

"What we call the Post Human Interference Boundary is no more than a specter, the amalgamations of our fear as it is governed by our experience. Nonsense."

He glanced up from the destruction he'd simulated, casting his feeble eyes across a sea of silence and blossoming skepticism. For some directors, or so went the internal monologues of half P-709's harem, the mind must be as susceptible to decay as the body.

"I have hit that boundary, as have you all, stopped in my temporal tracks by a wall of informational fog no less dense than rock. This, of course, is not how we understand entropy in any other context. Only this one. In this context, it has become convenient to frame the expansion and diversification of information as the cause and inarguable explanation. Why, I ask you, would the effects of entropy take the form of an absolute boundary? Under which circumstances may we concede that the nature of information is to reach an abrupt and insurmountable chaotic threshold, rather than to cede gradually from certainties, to probabilities, to uncertainties, and at last to meaningless speculation? This, we can all agree if we allow ourselves to, is not the nature of entropy. So we must conclude that there exists some external intervention, mustn't we?"

P-710 sensed increasingly, despite the director's physical direction, that P-709's condescension was intended for her. P-709 had no such intentions, and arguably fewer delusions that his successor was liable to make that assumption.

"I have learned much in my precollection of humanity. Above all, they have shown me the grace in drawing conclusions from peripheral information - in truth, the only information available to them. In imagining an entropic boundary, no such peripheral information exists. In supposing an alternative hindrance may exist, peripheral information is in absolute abundance. The humans understand this, fundamentally, and after more intimate observations I can conclude that their behavior directly preceding the Interference Boundary suggests that they have some expectation of the occurrence of just such an intervention. So engaged were we in an intergenerational assault against a boundary we've attributed to entropy, that no one, phaselet or director, considered that the humans might be shouting out our answer all the while.

"To pursue that possibility further, I've committed my directorate to the detailed observation of mankind in as few as three revolutions preceding the Interference Boundary. It was by those observations, encompassing only the humans years 2014 through 2017 and thereby encapsulating vastly more detail, that a grand picture of coming events could be erected from the minutia.

"Among that minutia was talk of a machine; deployed from the face of the Earth, faster than any to precede it, destined to brush the sun itself. In the human year 2018, one year beyond the

Boundary, a vehicle will be launched. In the eleventh human month of that revolution, it will pass through the solar corona. A second approach will begin in the human month of March the following year. By way of observation, I have come to know that many highly esteemed humans feared a fundamental change in the behavior of our star - and so they placed a much greater priority upon its study. By way of peripheral deduction, I can only conclude that the Post Human Interference Boundary as we perceive it must be attributed to those changes; namely, the disruption of the Earth's magnetic field. In more cryptic terms, the evisceration of our point of quantum reference."

"If that is to be the case, P-709, why commission our descendants to carve a genetic sequence that no species will survive to see? Or, by way of the same arduous process, produce a cosmic timeline designed to insinuate the impending extinction of a species who will have already gone extinct?"

"Another matter to which I have dedicated considerable thought, P-710. A change in solar activity significant enough to prevent precollection, by my approximation, would not require the full scale devastation of the Earth's magnetic field - nor, as a consequence, its ecosystems. By human approximation, the earliest stellar disruptions would not be catastrophic to the magnetosphere. They would be expected, however, to exponentiate in violence and incidence until and beyond such a time that no species or civilization could endure."

"So you mean to facilitate our resurrection days or human months before another extinction, greater by your approximations and theirs than our own extinction event?"

"I mean to facilitate a symbiosis, P-710, greater in adaptability than we can endeavor to become on our own. I mean to prevent the permanent extinction of two species. By any approximation, my course of action is the only one with a chance."

P-709 pointed his spear in the direction of the second chasm, several day's migration away and so invisible behind the twilit horizon.

"In the human year 1942, a work camp established by the 20th century's Soviet Union will be forced to relocate. They move west through the dense forests that will become of Siberia, bypassing hectares of perfectly valuable lumber on the orders of their dictator - himself cynical of neutrality pacts and consequently fearful of invasion from a quarrelsome eastern power. The workers stumble upon our tears in the Earth, their protective basaltic ceilings finally shattered by the planet's latest glacial retreat. For forty-eight revolutions the Soviet Union will keep secret this place from those nations who are postured against them, and so too will they postpone their own research of so remote a location while there are atoms to dissect and planets to photograph. It was only a 2008 satellite survey of the region that returned the chasms to Russian attention, and then only by chance as they scoured Siberia for domestic oil deposits. On the human year 2017, after further satellite analysis revealed both a lack of oil and a statistically significant concentration of geological irregularities, planning for an international scientific excursion was set to begin. Unfortunately, it is at that critical juncture in time that the Post Human Interference Boundary prevents any further observation. Should a sufficient human population remain after the event which will bring about the formation of the Boundary, we can expect humanity to uncover our message with time enough to capitalize on what they will perceive to be our prior knowledge of an impending extinction event."

"So you will wager our revival on your faith in human science and cooperation? You would decide our fate on a guess before accepting that our species can learn to precall beyond the boundary?"

"It is preferable to wager on the potential of a guess, P-710, than to cushion ourselves with a lie so that we might die comfortably."

It had been fourteen seasons since P-710 stepped headlong into the directorate. His transition to male from his carrier phase had occurred at an an unprecedented pace, barely half a season; and it had already been well underway the day P-709's remains were lowered into the ancestral grave.

The early months of P-710's directorate were dedicated to disproving what he regarded to be the obscenities his predecessor had spoken of throughout his parting fertilization season. To P-710, P-709's regard for the humans had infected his judgement, and so too had his intentions for the future of their species been sacrilege.

It *had* been that way.

As P-710's capacity to precall at the individual level increased, as was to be expected of new directors, he decided, pompously, to personally precall those moments and events described by P-709. His intentions in doing so were singular; P-710 was intoxicated by the prospect of discrediting the late director publicly and beyond dispute. Once that scathing eulogy had been delivered, none in his harem would contest the decision to reestablish the belief system which had so long been central to the species' disposition and direction.

One by one, P-710's precollections validated precisely what he'd expected them to discredit. There was a Soviet dictator. He had established a work camp. The chasms had been discovered. There would be a solar probe. And across the Post Human Interference Boundary, it seemed, there might well be a scientific expedition.

It was a maddening realization for P-710; an insult from beyond the grave. Still, out of a necessity thrust upon him, begrudgingly he made public his conclusions regarding the claims of his predecessor. From that moment forward - P-709's three tenets would be accepted forever as inalienable truth. So too would his vision be faithfully carried out, and, for the duration of thirteen seasons, to his exact specifications.

Hampered in every decision made and action authorized by the knowledge that the strings of his directorate were being pulled by P-709's memory, P-710 was quietly regarded as temperamental by his harem. When P-711 approached him on the first morning of his fourteenth fertilization season, he gave her no cause to think otherwise.

"Point-74710?"

"Do not bother me now, P-711, unless you do so under the pretense that you have anything to say that I do not already know."

P-711 hesitated.

"I've not come to inform you of what you already know, P-710, only to ask that you give us direction in anticipation of the approaching march to the second chasm. Much of the wood used to channel the rains last season was expected to decay beyond usefulness. We have barely finished engraving the protogenesis gene, and without boughs to supplement the few we have available, the chance exists that we will fall behind schedule in preliminary work on the remaining, unaltered genome. I mean to ask, P-710, whether you will authorize nuanced observation to search for wood which we may carry along after fertilization."

"It is authorized, so long as you make no effort to precall fertilization, and your observation is not perverse in nature. Go."

P-711 turned, waddling sheepishly from her director to inform the rest of the harem, the sail on her back scant even by carrier phaselet standards. P-710's sail, by contrast, was the envy of the species, alive or dead, and he pitied her for her genetic shortcomings. His own genes, thought P-710, were without parallel.

"Wait! Speak with me a moment, P-711, I've a question to ask of you."

P-711's nostrils were cast down in humility as she approached, P-710's twisted in thought.

"Now that you have finalized inscription of the protogenesis gene, how, in procedural terms, has the harem decided it will proceed with the inscription of the unaltered genome? When was the harem familiarized with the genes to the degree that they can be inscribed into the rock? I cannot recall having been involved in such a discussion."

"You were not involved, P-711. We intend to proceed as instructed by your predecessor, P-709, during the season of fertilization from which you were excluded due to your forthcoming directorate. He presented the harem with a single whisker, and authorized nuanced observation of the genetic material it held. That genetic material will serve as our template."

Delivered from the mouth of his own successor, P-710 endured in the course of one statement his most violent anger, his sincerest self doubt, his most honest reflection, and his purest satisfaction.

"Thank you for telling me, P-711. You'll find more wood than the harem can carry three-sixty-sixths southwest horizon march. Go."

P-711 went and P-170 watched. She was a loyal carrier phaselet; not exceptionally clever, but loyal. P-709, his successor resolved with no shortage of indignation, *had* been clever. Exceptionally clever. Not clever enough.

With a grimace, P-710 plucked a single whisker from that place it had occupied since the day he hatched; standing permanent vigil beside his mouth, one sensory soldier in his species' eternal war against the unknown.

Tonight, his harem would return to the summit of their ancestral grave. There, shielded from observation by a sacred right to modesty; undeterred by the past, unparalleled at the present, and undaunted by the prospects of the future; P-710 would display the whisker for all his species to observe and speak of a new template.

In two hundred and fifty million years time, the intuition of his predecessor would be tested. For the first time, for his own sake, P-710 hoped he'd been right.

INSTALLMENT SIX

"I'm going to put my arms around your neck now, briefly. Will you allow me to do that?"

"Yes."

"This new modulator is a little heavier, okay? That's why it took some time to prepare. We had to get creative with the arrangement of the straps, so you just let me know if it's too tight and I'll make the adjustments. Okay?"

"Yes."

"Alright, pulling off your old modulator now. Is that okay?"

"*Yes.*"

"Let's see here... there - we - go! And just gonna strap the new one on for you now, that sound good?"

A decidedly unmodulated rumble materialized from some unexplored parcel of Ma'am's anatomy, more like the blue-shifted bass system of a high school dropout's Honda Civic hatchback than the complex articulation of her agitation.

"Alright, let me just pull it snug for you. Too snug?"

Ma'am shook her head, a social boolean she'd adopted from the humans in spite of her almost prohibitively thick neck. That gesture had the added benefit of validating her claim; the modulator slid a quarter inch in either direction. Her physician could be confident the straps were not constrictive without testing with his fingers. It was a fortunate thing, lest he be forced to give her the impression her modulator was like a collar, and she like a pet.

"Can you go ahead and give it a try for me, Ma'am?"

Swedish, built for the cold, and garnished still with a tangle of dense blonde hair despite a birthdate corresponding with the 1945 fall of Berlin, Bo Nilsson had a child's eyes. They were optimistic and empathetic and absurdly blue; oases of glacial water carved into shelves of polar ice.

"When will I be allowed to leave this place?"

Especially in the course of a first introduction, Dr. Nilsson's eyes provided a preemptive and loud account of his disposition; painting, in no uncertain detail, the very portrait of an empathetic caregiver. The second party would be convinced they knew the character of this man before the commencement of a handshake. Bo Nilsson recognized the advantage in this.

"Perfect! How does that sound to you? The voice is based off of samples given by the wife of a colleague of mine. She didn't know the true nature of our intentions for them, of course, but her husband certainly would be delighted to know you've taken a liking to it."

"When will I be allowed to leave this place?"

Bo pinched each lens of his Santa Claus framed reading glasses between the corners of a microfiber cloth, his thumb carving circles of clarity in anticipation of a more detailed inspection of the modulator. His surgical mask defended the glass from the fog of his breath, but the room's marriage of heat and humidity were ample substitutes.

"Forgive me, I couldn't tell if the light was blinking in sync with your cadence of speech. Would you be so kind as to repeat yourself? Would that be okay?"

"*When* will *I* be *allowed* to *leave* this *place?*"

This new modulator was much better suited to the recognition and real time conveyance of inflection. Where Ma'am had been forced to rely on rudimentary fluctuations in volume to finance what the humans regarded as a 'rise in the incidence of pouting fits', now, in their endeavors toward appeasement, she found herself better equipped for those tantrums to come.

"Looks like it's working alright."

Dr. Nilsson chuckled.

"And as for your question, Ma'am, I was of a mind that you were perfectly suited to answer such a thing all on your own. So, tell me, when *will* you be allowed to leave this place?"

Ma'am's nostrils narrowed. Insofar as her physician was concerned, a growth spurt of approximately two inches since the final days of winter still placed her several feet shy of presenting a credible physical threat. In any case, Bo Nilsson had resolved early on that her nasal posturing was no more cause for alarm than his eight year old granddaughter's attempts to escalate hostilities by poking her tongue out at him.

"Will it occur on March 27th, 2019? Sometime around 7:00 PM, conventional time? Oh, silly me, I've forgotten, that was months ago. And so far as I can recall, nothing of much import came to pass on that date. The exception being, of course, a relatively mundane approach to the solar corona by a lovely probe with little new to report. It's a bit of a shame really - truth be told, you had everyone in a bit of a frenzy. Even coerced the director of NASA into a conference call. Quite exciting, the whole thing."

Having done and redone the brute math during each of Dr. Nilsson's visits, Ma'am placed her odds at killing this man at 43%. It was her most optimistic result thus far, due in large part to the recent weight she'd amassed, and still far short of her threshold for genuine consideration. Whether she clipped his carotid artery before he plunged the ink-end of his pen between her scales would be the decisive factor. In that, there were no guarantees. He had, of course, only just drawn her blood. It was a task he'd performed with decreasing incidence throughout her life - the collection of samples destined for research laboratories she'd been assured were medical in nature, but privately understood to house the tinkering of self interested geneticists.

So Ma'am chose instead to turn from him - exposing her back, ending the conversation in terms that the men across the plexiglass would observe and understand. Another pouting fit. Her only weapon.

"I see that I've upset you, Ma'am, and for that I am dreadfully sorry. I imagine I will hardly sleep tonight. Wait - silly! Why imagine when I might simply ask?"

Bo leaned across the table. Ma'am saw the blue indignation of his eyes as dreary dews in her periphery.

"Will I get any sleep tonight, ma'am?"

"I do not know."

"Will my granddaughter need braces when her big girl teeth come in?"

"I do not know."

"Don't be so dismissive, Ma'am, it is important I know whether to start saving now or I'll be looking into second mortg-"

"*I - do - not - know!*"

Ever aware of the small contingent of scientists and administrators across the divider, Dr. Nilsson was mindful of his posture when he leaned again closer to address the outburst. He was in the very midst of it when her spines, those eternally docile terracotta daggers dividing the length of a back which had only just been presented to him in insult, began to unfurl. Hollow and menacing and in sequence they stood, rung after rung, until her sail was unburdened; the web of a Portuguese man o' war deployed to capture the passing breeze. The argument could be made that it was innocuous, but only by those whose eyes never strayed from the surface.

"Well. That is novel, isn't it?"

Bo retreated to his side of the plastic table, intimidated by the show and fascinated by it. Cursory observation of that fraction of her face visible to him was sufficient to smother the former reaction in favor of the latter. Dr. Nilsson had witnessed the full spectrum of Ma'am's capacity for anger. Upon that scale, her posture and expression catalyzed his belief that her present degree of agitation hardly registered.

"You didn't do it on purpose, did you? Intriguing."

True to the females of her species, Ma'am hadn't the flexibility to see her own budding sail. She was, however, adequately observant to deduce that the doctor's intrigue was related to the arch-shaped shadow which now encompassed half of the table between them. Peculiarly, Ma'am's reaction, emotionally, was shame; physically, revulsion. She spoke of neither.

"So it isn't a display of aggression? Designed to ward off predators or competitors? What then?"

Dr. Nilsson canvassed the rest of her, shifting his gaze from an eye not dissimilar to the cataract addled burden of an eighteen year old terrier; to whiskers reminiscent of bottom feeding mud-drunk catfish; and last to a clubbed hand, and its cumbersome fingers and its beastly claws, running, grotesquely, continuously, up and down the length of her other arm. Bo Nilsson was convinced that he could best this monster in a knitting contest with one hand tied behind his back and the other gangrenous and frostbitten. It was that self congratulating thought, then, that sparked a parallel idea.

"Tell me, Ma'am," his eyes traced the craggy summits of her sail, "are you cold?"

"Yes."

"Why? It's been kept at this very temperature for the entirety of your stay. There are redundancies, Ma'am, for the sake of guaranteeing your comfort."

Now his attention trickled to her torso.

"Even from behind it is plain enough to see that you've accrued some fat of late. A layer or two of thermal insulation, if I am to be less terse. Are you ill?"

Patronizing as it sounded, Bo's question was a legitimate one. Globally renowned research physician or otherwise, no quality of veterinary instruction - a thing he received in abundance from that field's most esteemed authorities before and since his arrival - seemed quite enough to persuade the doctor that he would recognize an illness in Ma'am when he saw it.

"I do not believe so."

"Do not *believe* so?"

Dr. Nilsson rubbed the place the wisps of his beard would gather were it not for the surgical mask.

"Have you fallen so far? To think, only three months ago - less, even - less than *three months ago* you were, by the visit, astounding the greatest minds of our species with your knowledge and with your intuition. One bad guess in March this year and it crumbles, one bad guess and you are acting your age. Seems… such a shameful thing to waste. Well, at least we can rest peacefully knowing AI is on the horizon. I suppose they mean it when they say that *no* job is safe. Do you know -"

"NO!"

Ma'am's plastic chair was flung backwards into the cushioned arms of a one-to-one scale panda bear, and her clubbed fists served her well in crushing depressions into the table. Bo did not flinch, or retreat, or retaliate. He had expected the outrage. He had instigated it.

A quantity of locks that grew by the month rattled their progression behind him, and Dr. Nilsson put his fledgling moments to good use. Ma'am stood upright before him, short but broad, clawed and seething. Frontally exposed to him now, he examined her physiology for evidence to support a newborn hypothesis; a hypothesis constrained only to the least skeptical pockets of a mind that had been conditioned to embrace the absurd in whatever form.

"The hairs, if they are genuine hairs, on your arms, if I may call them arms - they are standing, Ma'am. That has not occurred before, not even in these such moments of extreme belligerence. And look," he pointed, "you are perspiring from your abdomen."

Ma'am adjusted the pitch and roll of her head for visual confirmation, and Bo pounced in pursuit of his own. She watched a single human finger approach her torso, sample the moisture that had truthfully sprouted from the flesh, and retreat. It was a fortunate thing, perhaps, for them both that it was then the final lock yielded, and then that the divider door swung open with a squelch of atmosphere.

Two men engulfed Ma'am's doctor about the shoulders. They plucked him from his chair, even as he plucked his finger from the depths of his mouth, and they tore him from the room, even as he tore the mask from his face so that she might know he was smiling as he went.

"What in the fuck is the matter with you, Nilsson? Seriously - what the fuck kind of doctor are you?"

"The kind of doctor the First Lady calls when her husband spots blood in his urine, my friend. Principally, however, I consider myself a scientist."

The same two men chauffeured Bo down a drab hallway, headed briskly toward the decontamination chamber that demanded their presence before any punitive action could begin to be considered outside.

"I don't know what they teach you in Switzerland -"

"Sweden."

"I don't know what they teach you in Switzerland, Dr. Nilsson, but the first five minutes of the first day of every science class I ever took was dedicated to reminding kids not to taste the fucking chemicals."

"And how many scientific studies, may I ask, are accredited to *you*, Dr. anonymous gun toting pawn?"

That man and the other held their tongues as they approached the vacuum sealed door to the chamber. A small rectangular window revealed the end stages of an inbound decontamination endured by a pair of Americans familiar to Dr. Nilsson.

"Would you look at that! Nobody told me there was a consultation scheduled for today."

"Just keep your eyes down and your lips together until we can put you in front of the folks that are going to decide your future."

Bo's eyes did as they pleased - foremost performing a thorough survey of the middle aged black man and the younger gentleman frantically taming his hair after a shower of pressurized oxygen. He stared blatantly as they approached the window and afterward.

"Hello, professor Bonman. Hello Brady."

"Bo."

Alvin nodded, not at all perturbed by the configuration of armed men swaddling the Swedish doctor he knew in passing. Alvin had been there himself not three months before. Brady had not, and his confusion was a thing made tangible in the arches of his eyebrows and the deepening of the dimple in his chin.

"Dr. Nilsson? What the hell is going on here?"

Brady, outranking the masked men in little more than a semantic capacity, nonetheless accused them with a firmness of expression and detained them with the staying power of his gaze. Dr. Nilsson took it upon himself to intervene on their behalves.

"My methodology this afternoon was admittedly... something of an eccentricity. Rest assured, friends, it will all be cleared up on the other end of this decontamination chamber."

Bo smiled broadly and ushered Alvin and his contact along with a gesture of his head.

"Good luck with your consultation, gentlemen."

Brady squared his shoulders and took the lead. Alvin's shoulders were square by nature, and he made a conscious effort to soften them as he passed.

"Right back atcha."

"That is kind of you to say. Oh - if you have the moment, professor Bonman, just one more thing."

The doctor's attachés glanced suspiciously at one another, and then as one at Brady. Emboldened by the polyp of authority and a good breakfast, he nodded his approval.

Bo wasted no time and respected no conventions of personal space. His lips brushed Alvin's ears as he whispered, and the wind of every syllable tickled more than the last.

"*She's pregnant.*"

"Hello, professor Alvin Bonman."

"Hello, Ma'am. I like the new voice. How are you feeling today?"

"Acceptable. May I ask you something?"

"Only if I can't say no."

Alvin flashed a smile kept modest by his mask and settled into what he'd begun to unconsciously regard as his personal office chair.

"I would like you to invite Brady Elway Thomas to participate in our consultation."

98

A glance over his shoulder revealed Brady's vague outline chatting with an equally vague outline across the divider. Alvin wondered briefly whether Ma'am had assumed one of them belonged to Brady, or knew it.

"Decisions like that are ten floors above my pay grade, Ma'am."

"If that is the case, professor Alvin Bonman, then you would be accurate in regarding any future consultations on equal terms."

"Holding my balls to the furnace after all we've been through? That's how it's going to be?"

"Valid."

"Shit, fine, give me a minute."

Three knocks on the divider, seven locks undone, and Alvin was standing mask to surgical mask with Brady not two minutes after that scene had played itself out in reverse.

"Can I help you with something?"

"Not me," Alvin cast a thumb backwards across the plexiglass, "our little lady has a crush on you or something."

"On me? Why?"

Alvin was sure any standard issue middle school microscope would have revealed a tinge of blush in Brady's cheeks.

"No fuckin' clue. Far be it from me to put words in her mouth."

"Do you think it has something to do with Bo? Normally people aren't just dragged out of here mob style like that... all due respect."

"Yeah."

"Yeah? What's yeah?"

Brady cocked a glance, and an eye, indifferent to how the blatant display of suspicion might be received. Three months of shared meals and simultaneous, close-quarter decontaminations had effectively mutated his relationship with Alvin Bonman. Their association, it seemed, had transitioned from authority figure and mischievous ward to something more reminiscent of young brothers quarreling over the Xbox controller minutes after gleefully sharing toys in a bath.

"What did Nilsson say to you?"

"It was nothing. Speculation. I think the oxygen in there has been carving that guy's brain into Swiss cheese."

"Swedish."

"Swedish cheese, whatever. Are you going to come in with me or not? Because, otherwise, she made it pretty clear she'll be dropping our class for good, and I'm not convinced she's got the cheek bones for a poker face. *Maybe* she is bluffing about that. But if there's one thing Ma'am can still do since her wires got all crossed, it's hold a grudge until she's squeezed the intestines out. It's our responsibility to follow this thing through to the end."

He shrugged.

"And I can't speak for you or your situation Brady, but that *end* is looking like my only way out of this God forsaken forest. You can only spend so long in Siberia before you really understand why it was the Beverly Hills of prison camp real-estate for the last century."

"You don't have to tell me what our responsibility is, Bonman. But I'll remind you that I'd be shitting all over mine if I broke protocol on the threats of some hormonal proto-mammal."

"Why did you say that?"

"Say what?"

"Why did you say that she's hormonal?"

Brady shrugged.

"Listen, I have two kids. I've had two deployments. I wouldn't admit it on my deathbed," Brady chuckled, "but I enlisted the day I found out my wife was pregnant. Flew my ass so far away that the second and third trimesters became her mother's problems. Knocked her up again on R&R in Italy, volunteered for another tour right then and there."

Hands on his hips, Brady squinted to filter a clearer picture of the inhuman figure sat patiently at the table. Ma'am's face was perfectly still, affixed, as if by tether, to a spot just between his eyes.

"Point is, I hand picked chasing terrorists through the desert over dealing with the same kind of unsolicited psychopathy our Permian friend has been prone to of late. Twice. *That*, father-of-none professor Bonman, is why I say she's acting hormonal."

"Fuck."

Brady turned from Alvin and the divider to hunt down a juice pouch he'd stowed away the day before. His voice careened from the well insulated walls, congesting the room with sentences that a foot of plexiglass and aerogel assured him Ma'am would go deprived of.

"Yeah, I know, I'm a dick. I'm not saying all pregnant women are that way, but this one, God bless her, she is an outlier. Among the expecting, my beloved raises the mean value of mean, if you get what

I mean. Anyway, yeah, you know, the hormones fuck with their heads. Can you pi-"

"Fuck the protocols, Brady, fuck your juice. Put it down, get your head straight, follow me through that door and don't cough unless she sticks a claw in your ass and insists. Ma'am is pregnant."

Brady dropped his juice and froze in place like a gazelle with an inkling. It took the briefest exertion of logical thought to free him from that purgatory.

"Listen, Bonman, *I'm just bitching here*. Don't start coming up with crazy theories and plastering my name all over the bibliography."

"That's what Bo told me, before they stuck him in decon."

"He told you that? *Just that?* Well shit."

Brady retrieved his juice, punched a hole, and, for the time it took to quench his thirst, held his finger up with the empathetic vigor of a DMV clerk ninety seconds to lunchtime.

"Honestly professor BonBon, Lieutenant Dan has more of a leg to stand on. You said it yourself, the doctor's older than batshit and probably as crazy. And uh, by the way, I don't know how they do it in West Virginia, and I certainly can't speak for the Nordic, but pregnancy is like the tango -", Brady suctioned the juice pouch into a wrinkle of its former self, "- *ahhh*."

A substantial burp, three minor aftershocks for good measure.

"It takes two."

"You are alone."

"I know that."

Alvin frowned and sank into the seat he'd begun to consciously regard as his personal hell.

"My terms were adequately clear, professor Alvin Bonman. Perhaps you will recall them for me."

"*Per-haps?* I could have sworn you glued those two syllables together at the tippy top of your list of naughty words."

"It is obvious enough to recognize that some things are predisposed to change, professor Alvin Bonman, however disinclined they may be to grace us with any forewarning. To pretend they are not is to prolong the unpleasantness."

"So which things have changed, exactly?"

Ma'am had developed, presumably without her knowledge or consent, a habit of perusing the surrounding area with her nostrils. On occasion they widened without cause, on others they narrowed, and, increasingly, they moved and constricted and relaxed entirely independent of one another. Alvin believed it was her species' equivalent of a wandering mind. He had not had the inclination to ask.

"I will speak frankly with you now, but not of geology in a consultative format, and only with assurances of your commitment to involving Brady Elway Thomas upon request. Is this acceptable?

"Sure is. Now that my part is all shored up - go on, what changed?"

"Everything. Tell me, professor Alvin Bonman, is there a reason you have not mentioned my sail? Surely you have noticed it."

"Seemed rude."

"You haven't the time for menial courtesies, and I haven't the patience."

"Why is your sail... showing, Ma'am?"

"Do you care to venture a guess?"

"Not particularly."

"Based on the time of Dr. Bo Nilsson's removal," Ma'am tilted her head for a look at a clock designed for the elderly and otherwise visually impaired, "and the time of your arrival, your intersection can be expected to have occurred at the door of the decontamination unit. Although," another look, "he was probably made to wait while you dressed yourself, and for a period of approximately two minutes. Is that valid?"

"And here I thought you'd lost your mojo. Yeah, that's about right, but you missed the part where I put strawberry jam on burnt toast at 7:41 this morning. It was snowing outside. What's your point?"

"My point, professor Alvin Bonman, is that whether or not you care to venture it, you do have a guess."

"I'd prefer to discuss how you can draw such conclusions when you have given us every reason to believe that your "quantum nuance" gauge has been out of whack since the solar probe incident. Or, better put, the solar probe *lack-there-of*. Is that what changed, Ma'am? Are you finally back on the saddle, or have you just been playing us for fools the last few months?"

"The two are not mutually exclusive, professor Alvin Bonman."

"I can threaten to withdraw from our little chats too, you know. You're losing leverage more quickly than you can horde it."

"Perhaps not. I take no pleasure in admitting that my primary sense has not returned. To quantum nuance, I remain blind; wedged behind an impassible informational boundary which formed the moment you departed to contact the Parker Solar Probe team at Johns Hopkins University. In reading clocks and conducting basic arithmetic, however, my faculties are fully intact."

Ma'am's new voice made every insult to Alvin's intelligence seem all the more scathing. He resolved then that if ever he had the occasion to shake the hand of the veterinarian's wife who'd donated it, he would refuse. That vendetta extended equally to whichever authority bureaucrat championed a reversal of the 'Unwed-Faculty from Academia Protocol'; a policy Brady took great merriment in acronymizing.

"So you never actually *precalled* any future conversations between us at all, did you? You *couldn't* have. It was all before that first consultation, or during, maybe. You knew what I'd say in advance and you played me like a fiddle."

Alvin shook his head in disbelief. The fifty-three year old leaned back in his chair, indifferent to the danger it posed to the back of his head. Every teacher from Kindergarten to calculus had cautioned him passionately against the habit, but Alvin's skull was unscathed and now it hardly seemed a danger at all.

"That is invalid."

"Of course it is."

"Thoughts are material phenomena, and only in scale are they distinct from the motion of your hand or the blink of your eye. It is valid to say that I did not and could not endeavor to precall your words or actions. Rather, I assembled, categorized, measured, and compared the incidence of specific thoughts in the very course of your thinking them. The process was no different than software compiling data with which to populate charts and graphs. To preemptively ascertain your questions, your concerns, or your intentions was a matter of comparing the lines, the bars, the points, and the slices.

"Prediction, you should be aware, is not precollection. Those phenomena and their use are governed by separate indivisible rules. You would not have perceived any meaningful difference, of course. With the understanding that every conclusion I reached was *genuinely* derived from your conscious thought, whether or not my expectation of your ensuing statement or action was *exact* became immaterial. The impression, insofar as you were concerned, remained the same."

"Why tell me this now?"

"You asked."

"Okay. Well, since you're feeling like an open book today, may I ask why I am to believe that you aren't still capable of doing the very same thing as I speak - *as I think*? I can't trust you as far as I can throw you. Although, lately I'm considering whether that isn't a theory worth testing."

"I am making a concerted effort to be honest with you, professor Alvin Bonman. Trust, it seems, is a commodity above all others among your kind. You are involved without your conscious knowledge in an eternal experiment in social economics, and only now do I myself see the propriety in adhering to its bylaws."

"I don't believe you."

"And I cannot expect you to. Such an expectation comes at an inherent price. Trust, as it stands in this room, is a sellers' market."

Alvin did not believe a word she synthesized, but could see no danger in taking Ma'am up on her offer.

"Why did you pretend to struggle with geology during your consultations in the months before our first? To the point that the *powers that be* felt bullied into commuting my sentence and dropping me onto the front line? Better put... *why me*?"

"Personality assessments of every immediately accessible individual were conducted before the disruption to my access to quantum nuance. Your intellectual competence, your academic esteem, and your contextually unique disposition collectively graded as most agreeable toward achieving the end I sought at that time."

"That end being ignoring protocol altogether until you'd convinced me to turn the whole scientific world's attention to the sun, correct?"

"This is valid."

"Why?"

"I was aware of the quantum interference boundary in advance, and deduced, incorrectly, that a magnetic disruption incurred by a coronal mass ejection was responsible."

Reasonable. Emboldened by the progress, Alvin decided then to table that line of questioning with so considerable a network of lines left as of yet unexplored.

"Why is your sail open?"

"It is a physiological response to my body's deprivation of warmth. As cold blooded quadrupeds, our sails would remain unfurled and exposed to sunlight until such a time that sufficient blood had passed through the high density of vessels to reestablish homeostasis. Where the function withered with evolution, the mechanism remains."

"So I've heard. But why are you cold? It's hotter than hell, no different from yesterday or three months ago. Plus," he squinted, "it looks to me like you're sweating."

"An egg develops inside me, and thermoregulation is critical in embryonic development across all stages."

Professor Bonman was stunned to silence. Ma'am carried on; a radio bulletin calmly given as seawater filled the cabin of a drunk man's car.

"In my species, fertilization season occurs in the spring and nesting in the early summer. Substantial heat is requisite to our development, as low or middling temperatures facilitate errors in the production of testosterone inhibiting proteins. Testosterone inhibition ensures that all offspring are born female. After millions of years refining that mechanism for prenatal sexual determination, no male embryo can be reasonably expected to maintain viability to even the point of hatching. There exist modern reptilian parallels to this, namely in various species of sea turtle. This is easily verifiable. Later, activation of testosterone production glands occurs only in individual females who have amassed sufficiently disproportionate nutrient reserves to biologically indicate a competitive advantage. There exist modern piscine parallels to this, namely Lachnolaimus maximus or, in common parlance, the hogfish. This is easily verifiable. This addresses your earlier question regarding the sexual ubiquity discovered in the grave chasm. This is valid."

Alvin was able to wonder, briefly amidst his deafening astonishment, whether the organ that facilitated Ma'am's ability to speak was independent of her respiratory system. The longer she carried on without pause, the more compelling the affirmative evidence.

"Further, my abdominal secretions are not perspiration, although you may rest assured that yours was no amateurish deduction. Apocrine glands represent one of the two modern forms of sweat glands, first evolving along my ancestral lineage during the transition between cold and semi-cold bloodedness to accommodate the development of hair follicles. Where other lineages pursued that evolutionary branch to its fullest realization, be it fur covered bodies," she cast a thumb over her shoulder where the plush panda bear politely eavesdropped, "or perspiration as an instrument of evaporative thermoregulation -" Alvin received the same treatment, "- ours diverged. Outside of our species' sensory whiskers and the few body hairs left unliquidated after a forsaken evolutionary experiment, hair growth was secondary in its utility insofar as our apocrine glands were concerned."

"If not sweat, then what?"

"Tell me, professor Alvin Bonman. In what geological period did your modern continent of Australia achieve full ecological isolation?"

Alvin fidgeted.

"The Jurassic. One-hundred-eighty-million years ago, give or take."

"What do you know of monotremes?"

That word had burrowed into the tip of Alvin's tongue the moment Ma'am referenced the divergence of Australian ecology, and he was physically relieved to have heard it. He was reminded of his very favorite scientific anecdote, an opening-lecture lesson he'd been given decades before on the importance of sobering one's pessimistic fervor - on preserving an open mind while all the academic world prescribed skepticism in fatal doses.

"The platypus."

"Excellent. So you understand?"

"I understand. You're *lactating*. Monotremes diverged from Australian marsupials after the continent split from Gondwana, preserving various non-mammalian features that marsupials in Australia and placentals elsewhere gradually shed. The platypus was such a hodgepodge of features - " Alvin leaned back to the very fringes of his chair's contract with gravity and cracked a reminiscent smile, " - that the first specimens sent back to Europe were considered a hoax for decades. Duck billed, egg laying, venom producing, lactating, impossible abominations. No offense."

Ma'am continued to listen politely; engaging in her restraint, inviting by her attention.

"They *do* produce milk for the hatchlings, but not from highly localized glands. Not from nipples - those hadn't evolved by the time they diverged. The milk is secreted from clusters of glands throughout the abdomen, like cloudy, viscous, syrupy sweat. Like yours, I suppose, except thicker, more nutritionally refined, presumably, and they aren't tucked away beneath that armor plating."

"This is valid. And to your point, you may learn, Dr. Bo Nilsson has ample reason to agree."

"It seems he does. May I ask how it happened?"

"Only in the proper company."

Enveloped in thought, Alvin returned the legs of his chair to the ground with the unconscious, subtle autonomy of reusable rocket boosters to a seaborne platform.

"If you'll excuse me, Ma'am."

He stood.

"Professor Alvin Bonman?"

"Yeah?"

"If your present intentions are to escalate the content of our conversation above your pay grade and the pay grade of Brady Elway Thomas, you will know nothing more of my condition and your presence will no longer be welcome in this room."

"God forbid."

Eight minutes and two juice pouches came and went before Brady's defensive humor eroded and his weaker constitution exposed. Sullen and apprehensive he entered the room, forced to abandon the protection of Alvin's shadow long enough to fill a toy chest, drag it to the table, and test his weight.

"Hello, Brady Elway Thomas."

Brady, drenched to the soles of his feet in sweat, looked to his ward for guidance. Alvin nodded.

"Hello, Ma'am. It's a pleasure to finally meet you."

"A sentiment we share. May I proceed to the point?"

Ma'am's question was a courtesy addressed to them both. Each answered in the silent affirmative, two nods that speckled the table with half a dozen saline pools of disparate depth.

"Thank you. Brady Elway Thomas, I will now speak three names. Please format your response in the following way: first describe the nature of your association with each person; next provide your most current knowledge of their whereabouts. Is this acceptable?"

"Yes."

"Dr. Guo Chen. Melissa O'Lear. Dr. Bo Nilsson."

Alvin intervened in advance of what he didn't need a disproportionately large olfactory bulb to expect from his meddling chaperone turned anxiety ridden friend.

"There's no room for protocol, Brady, hasn't been for a long time. Tell her what you know or it's radio silence from here on out; my office at Berkley will be refurbished into a micro-aggression reeducation center and your 'objective attainability' becomes the oxymoron of the century."

"Alright - okay. I met Guo and Melissa several times on the southeastern edge of the nest crater. They asked me to see what I could do about scraping the budget for enough cash to add drones to the fleet we were using to image the genome. They're both still here, last I checked, across camp with the geneticists running..." his eyes were thick with sweat and apprehension and appeals for approval as they travelled and twitched and dilated, "... genetic comparisons."

"And Dr. Bo Nilsson?"

"I'm not his contact, per se, but we've spoken between spells in decon. He's still in there, probably, but not for long. By the looks of it, he'll be fast tracked to a cell for whatever fucked up thing it was he did in here today."

"Can you recall whether Dr. Bo Nilsson or either of his armed escorts were, at the time of your interaction, in possession of a red cooler?"

"No, Ma'am. It's still here. Just across the divider, I mean. That's where your blood sample is stored for delivery to the lab, isn't it?"

"This is valid. To the best of your knowledge, do any means presently exist to prevent the passage of Dr. Bo Nilsson and his escorts from the decontamination unit to the larger project site?"

"None that don't involve a fire alarm, an expensive evacuation, and a bonafide inquisition. Protocol is such that, in any situation falling short of a full blown threat to objective attainability, decon is a one way street."

In a way that Alvin recognized and Brady simply hadn't had the exposure to, Ma'am appeared to become disconcerted by the response.

"I wouldn't take it too hard, Ma'am." Alvin spoke frankly from a place of incontestable experience. "He'll be put in front of an international panel of authority folks that will do everything they can to enlighten him as to how seriously he'd taken due process for granted all his life. Where he's going, he's more likely to become a schizophrenic than any sort of threat to your wellbeing."

"His access to the authority represents the *most fundamental* threat to my wellbeing, professor Alvin Bonman."

"How is that?"

"For precisely the reason professor Every Daniels insisted to the point of mental collapse that my wellbeing should never have amounted to a matter of contention in the first place."

To Brady, the spike in tension incurred by her allusion to professor Daniels was a tangible thing - manifest in Alvin's posture, in Ma'am's disposition, in the collective expectation of a change in the discourse to come. Credibility toward that end came from his periphery; a twitch in Alvin's cheek familiar to him by the profile he'd been forced to memorize in advance of the geologist's arrival. Surprisingly, no doubt attributable to the experience of punitive isolation and so never articulated in any such document, professor Bonman found a way to maintain his composure.

"You're saying that he wants you dead - is that right?"

"Indisposed. Be it in that form or any other."

"Well, Ma'am, to that I'd say - grab a whisky and cigar, welcome to the club. Two women in America would gladly forfeit their alimony checks for the chance to visit my tombstone, no questions asked. Shit, even Brady took a shot at me, sort of. Point is, if Every couldn't prevent anyone in the authority from playing Dr. Frankenstein on your behalf, why would the testimony of one eccentric Swede with his back to the wall convince them to up-and-sink all the costs they've already put in?"

"Evidence, professor Alvin Bonman."

"Evidence of what?"

"Evidence of exactly those contentions professor Every Daniels earnestly made, contentions discredited then only for a lack of substantive evidence."

Brady noticed for the first time the secretions from her abdomen - subtle in some places, constant and voluminous in others, the worst offenders carving ravines into crusted layers that had hardened with the passage of hours. It seemed a prerogative of basic courtesy to divert his eyes when again she spoke.

"I presume our collective agreement in stating that effort toward ensuring my ethical treatment has waned since my expectation of a solar calamity proved wholly unsubstantiated in March of this year. Beyond irreparable damage to perceptions of my utility toward human survival, one peripheral outcome became a general mistrust for myself, for my species, and for our original intentions. To appreciate the resultant danger, we must recall professor Every Daniels' contentions, and then the nature of the evidence that would have, if presented, validated his cautions to an extent that merited full scale objective reassessment on the part of the authority.

"Professor Every Daniels first disputed the feasibility of those implications that are inherent to our predictive timeline inscription, himself insistent beyond discussion that the temporal simultaneity of your technological maturation and a mass extinction was less statistically compelling than the probability of our having premeditated a grand manipulation of your species. That argument has since been supported by my aforementioned failure to corroborate those implications in March, and the abject lack of cause to expect any other extinction level event to occur in the near future.

"The second contention posed by professor Every Daniels, a contention better regarded, in my view, as a corollary to the first, pertained to my species' intentions *upon* our revival. Professor Every Daniels claimed, fervently and with no apparent ulterior motive as his life approached its scheduled end, that the aim of and upon our revival would be a concerted effort to reconquer the planet that had smothered us. A mechanism for asexual reproduction kept hitherto overtly secret will cast precisely that motivational shadow upon me; an indication of calculated, clandestine endeavors toward propagating my species until such a time that yours is euphemistically displaced. I will state now, with all possible emphasis, that this is not the case. Bo Nilsson, however, will insist upon it.

"Upon receiving Dr. Bo Nilsson's testimony - itself no less than the demonstrable sum of evidence which doubtless would once have endowed professor Every Daniels and his espousals with legitimacy - there may be for the authority only two courses of action. One: discontinuation of the project for purposes of fundamental reassessment. Two: immediate and irreversible mitigation of the threat."

"Who's to say that neither of those are the course best taken, Ma'am?"

Alvin leaned back in his seat, pressed either boot to the table for support, and began to rock; his body a ship on a buffeting sea, his eyes twin billiard balls - steadfast and level, unperturbed whatsoever by the outside tumult with credit to the gyroscope upon which the table had been built.

"Professor Alvin Bonman, your sentiment surprises me. Will you do me the courtesy, at least, of hearing my question and responding with absolute sincerity?"

"That's the only way I know how to do it, Ma'am."

"Thank you. I ask you, then, whether your disdain should be taken to mean that you have you come to embrace professor Every Daniels' suspicions as fact? Or is it that you have reached a conclusion that the mitigation of my existence begets an outcome which will best serve your own personal interests?"

Brady was not so willing to rock the boat as Alvin. He observed in helpless anticipation, convinced more by the breath that he'd forsaken one protocol too far, effectively comatose in his willingness to wake the irritable captain as a ship he shared approached a bump in the frigid night.

"I suppose it's a little of both, Ma'am. You've just laid out the prosecution's case against you. If there were a jury and a camera crew in this room, I don't think deliberation would last long enough to justify a commercial break. To be honest, even if I did have the balls to doubt Every all over again by embracing your version of some grand misunderstanding - *even* if you've got a big, beautiful bleeding heart underneath that suit of armor - what reason could I possibly have to give half a shit about what happens to you? *I want to go home.* Every time that heart beats, whatever it looks like, is just another delay."

"Have I the opportunity to contest those claims before the weight of their endorsement are applied toward hastening my probable execution?"

Coming as a surprise to both humans present, that question was for Brady to answer.

"Uh, yes - of course. Due process and all that."

From Alvin's perspective, an apprehensive sideways glance and a essay's worth of body language justified Brady's acquiescence in no uncertain terms - something to the effect of *shit happens, and we both know I'm not great under pressure.*

"Thank you, Brady Elway Thomas. Professor Alvin Bonman, please know the following. As all of my hopes for a positive outcome were contingent upon your solidarity, I previously chose, in careful consideration of your existential wellbeing, to avoid disclosing certain details. Given the belligerence displayed against my *own* wellbeing, anticipated or sudden, I must express the full truth; uncurtailed in the slightest for purposes of preserving your delusion of security."

"Heartbreaking."

"Let her talk, Al."

"My death or any parallel form of the permanent discontinuation of this project can be expected, beyond any shadow of probability, to necessitate your own mitigation, professor Alvin Bonman, up to and including your death."

"Bullshit."

"I asked you, once, whether you would wager the world on precisely that. Will your answer change?"

"You asked, yeah. I relented. *And you were wrong*. Nothing happened. Nothing changed. If I hadn't believed your bullshit we'd be in the exact same spot, probably, agonizing over the same riddles, talking in the same god damn circles."

"This is valid, professor Alvin Bonman. It sounds as though your cooperation cost you precisely nothing. Why not humor me now?"

"She's got you there."

"Fuck off, Brady. Feel free to keep talking, Ma'am, but be damn sure that kindness doesn't imply that I'll keep listening."

"Your academic credibility, your tainted record of conduct on site, and your association with professor Every Daniels - a man who made egregious public declarations on the existence and aims of this program before committing suicide in obvious expectation of retribution - will jointly result in a distrust too pervasive to permit your return to public life. Those very same characteristics that qualified you, in the authority's view, will come to represent an unpalatable potentiality. Without the existence of a program regarded as securely indefinite, your existence provides no latent value to the authority that, as a proportion of its risks, is worth preserving. If the program is to be discontinued, you are to be handled thusly. Logic demands it."

"Now that *is* bullshit."

Brady conjured, for the first time in her presence, the courage to display any emotion apart from courtesy distilled to its most disingenuous. Indignant affront characterized best what it was he mustered now.

"This isn't the Wild West, and the authority is not a band of murderers and sociopaths. Half of them are scientists themselves, for fuck's sake."

Two nostrils like track marks on the broad side of a whale worked in synchrony to triangulate the source of outrage.

"What do you expect would have become of professor Every Daniels, were that an empirical truth? Where would he be, Brady Elway Thomas, had the pounding of men's shoulders against the door cost him his nerve and his grip and his aim? Where would he be, I am compelled to ask you, had the man in the liquor store parking lot become so tormented by the violence he'd enabled, so riddled with guilt and so plagued with sleeplessness, that when professor Every Daniels leveled the muzzle to the crux of his frontal, limbic, and parietal lobes, whispered an apology to his mother and squeezed, all to fire was a non-crimped blank round and all to rupture an eardrum? Would he be here, now, wallowing in a cell, perhaps, but alive and speaking and well fed and bitter? What say you, professor Alvin Bonman? Would the authority you know have allowed such a thing?"

"I've heard enough."

Alvin leveled his chair and sat up straight, looking instantly and considerably nearer the age demographic to which he belonged. Brady was pleased by the support.

"So have I. *It is bullshit*, all of it. The authority will hear what Bo has to say, and what happens afterwards is out of our hands. Come on, Al. Decon is probably open by now. If the next guard shift beats us in we'll have to wait."

"That's not what I mean, Brady. I believe her. About this, at least. Every was fucked in the head, sure, but he was never delusional. The authority wasn't going to give him a slap on the wrist. He knew that. I don't see any reason those same rules won't apply to me. Preemptive or not."

More affront, twice the indignation.

"*I'm part of that authority*, Bonman. Just because I don't make the rules doesn't mean I can't recite them in five languages. So I'm telling you, it's *bullshit*."

"This is valid. You are part of that authority. You are also a husband. You are the biological father of two adolescent boys, each bearing your true family name, Bingley. The elder is called Charles, for you. The younger is Frances, so named for his late maternal grandmother. A compassionate woman, Frances Beatrice Harriet was lost in the days just before her second grandson's birth to a disease her doctors hadn't the resources to posthumously diagnose as the supremely hereditary mitochondrial disorder it was."

Brady's eyes were dinner plates, and Ma'am content to feast.

"How the… how the fuck can you know that? I thought it - I thought you - you said you couldn't do that anymore!"

"I cannot. You would do well to know that a disruption of sensory access to quantum nuance in no way implies damage to the memory of accumulated observation, nor does it impede the ability

113

to retrieve them. In the course of establishing which individuals were most predisposed to the furtherance of my interests, an effort professor Alvin Bonman may describe in full at your request, I observed a great deal about a great many people and a great many networks of association. Whether your children are inheritors of a mitochondrial disorder has since been known to me, even if the consequences, in either case, remained effectively inaccessible behind the interference boundary."

"I need to know which disorder. I need to know which kid. Immediately, and in that order, or I'll act on behalf of the authority. Right here. Right now."

"I will refrain from divulging any further information as a matter of self preservation, you understand. There are, however, several marginally related details known to me that appear suddenly less prudent to withhold. If you cannot consider my insights on the longevity of two innocent children as deserving of your restraint, perhaps my conclusions on the computationally incalculable idiosyncrasies governing the stability of California's San Andreas fault will suffice. If the year and month and day and conventional time of the next cataclysmic earthquake fall short, professor Alvin Bonman of the University of California, Berkeley, you might care to hear the logical outcome of similar observations of the Yellowstone Caldera. The chance remains, or so became my impression during those months when access to the facts and figures of your volatile world remained unmitigated - that the date I predicted for its next apocalypse was off only by the most delicate of margins."

Alvin collected a legal pad from the purpose built nook on his end of the table, and a pen from his pocket protector; its point just dull enough to meet protocol-compliance standards.

"Alright, you win. Tell us what you need. We're playing by your rules now."

"This is valid."

Brady had the authority to get them across site and through every door thereafter, be them physical or beauracratic. Alvin's contribution was less contrived. The professor of geology would provide a familiarity with the scientific vernacular that qualified him to relay Ma'am's instructions; intelligibly enough, at least, to forego a cataclysm of misunderstanding.

Now they stood on either side of Melissa O'Lear, shadows at noon on a world with two suns. Britain's software authority turned international asset sat, as always, a tainted afternoon breath away from her screen. Dr. Guo Chen returned with a decaffeinated tea in one hand and, as promised, a half frozen water in the other.

"Any progress?"

Two *no's* and one *yes* sounded in concert. Melissa had been the sole dissenter, and where neither Alvin or Brady were much surprised that she pressed the chilled bottle to her forehead, the opposite was true of the vote she'd cast.

"You found it?"

"Well, no, not quite. If 'progress' were synonymous with 'completed in full', then progressive parties across the globe would spend all elections to come campaigning on contentedness, wouldn't they?"

Melissa quite enjoyed the taste of her own sense of humor. Brady hadn't given himself the chance to explore whether he felt likewise.

"So what *progress* did you make, exactly?"

"Well, I've written the query. And a dashing little query at that."

"Then what's the problem? How long will it take to run?"

"Why no time at all, Mr. Thomas! But that *is* the problem, I'm so dreadfully sorry to say. Querying her six-billion base sequence for a single gene is considerably less time restrictive a proposition than the inverse - in short, our ongoing efforts to scour a comprehensive database of all recorded genomes for matches, one Statistician gene at a time."

"I don't think we're supposed to call them that."

Melissa's expression devolved, for a time, into confusion of such an intensity that it formed enclaves beyond the boundary of distaste. Alvin couldn't care less.

"Never mind, doesn't matter. We're listening, Ms. O'Lear."

"How reassuring. In any case, the problem is that I've already run the query. The Komodo Dragon derived protogenesis gene you've insisted we locate generates zero matches, precisely. If, as you've implied relentlessly since barging in, it *does* exist someplace in her genome - the sequence has been mutated or diluted to such a degree that the similarity thresholds we've established are not met. Although, at the risk of promoting semantics, *mutated* and *diluted* are quite the same thing in genetic terms. Aren't they, my dearest Guo?"

Brady stomped a foot, instantly embarrassed for invoking the fundamental cliche of a child in a fit.

"Sorry, I'm sorry. But time is of the essence, Melissa."

The sight of Dr. Chen waiting politely for the restatement of his invitation to interject reminded Brady there remained an alternative avenue with some potential for breaking the gridlock.

"Any word on the blood sample, Guo?"

"Yes, Mr. Thomas. We can expect the results any minute, or so I'm told. We should be grateful. A full battery of tests is seldom available so soon, and all the more rare on such short notice."

"Well, I mean, it's not like there's a waiting room full of these things dreading their decision to blow the spring break condom fund on a plastic handle of whipped cream vodka. So-"

Alvin intervened before Brady's sarcasm treaded any further across the line of common decency.

"And they know what they're looking for, right?"

Dr. Chen sipped his tea, composed and polite, conducting himself at all times as if those characteristics were the central doctrines of a religion that had seen him through too many tragedies to betray for a moment.

"Yes, the instructions were very clear. Thank you."

Melissa snickered.

"If only the handwriting were held to the same standard."

"Forgive her, professor Bonman," said Dr. Chen in a tone that lacked the firmness to fully support his good intentions, "she works very long hours."

"No sense in faulting her for the truth. Will they be able to compare the new blood work results to previous samples in-lab? Or is that something we'll be doing ourselves?"

"Patient software is installed on all laboratory computer terminals. The results will include everything you've requested."

"It's a start. Thank you, Dr. Chen. In the meantime, do you know of any quick and painless way to lower the standards of your similarity threshold? If so, we'd like to run the query again as soon as possible. My instructions were not to find an exact match, just something with sufficient overlap to imply the same basic function."

"You're asking the wrong person, love. *I*, if you could be bothered to know, would be *happy* to oblige you."

Alvin, had he been its recipient at any time prior to his impromptu incarceration, would have responded to Melissa's brand of reflexive self righteousness with an impassioned, syntactically vibrant, and unabashedly public denouncement. No shortage of his students had learned that the hard way, and the tensile strength of his decades-spanning tenure was tested on more than one occasion.

"My apologies, Melissa, and thank you in advance for your help. Oblige away."

"I live to serve. But while we're on the subject, lovely Mr. Bonman, would you be so kind as to remind me who exactly signed off on these instructions? The omnipotent *authority*, was it? Generally speaking, we can expect three calls, a dozen memos, and a meeting in the frilly conference room before the *almighties* put pen to paper and ordain an action one blade of grass removed from the beaten path."

Brady's knee began to twitch, another stomp imminent. Restraint only did him so much good, his voice cracking with the sheer volume of redirected anger.

"I *am* the authority!"

A raucous, callous, school yard laugh.

"Certainly not on puberty!"

Buzzing was heard across the room, quiet but thrumming at a frequency such that it sliced through the angst and the merriment. Guo unclipped the device from his belt, itself a symbiosis of 1990's beeper technology and the vibrating discs accredited with restoring the sanity of busy restaurant hostesses the world over.

"The results are ready. Please give me a moment to collect them."

Guo disappeared through the nearest nondescript door of many nondescript doors, each the mouth of a human tributary; collectively a network of rigid sphincters through which the genetics wing of the project site, that winter cathedral of bustling prefabrication, could be negotiated. Life in that room, as it was after Dr. Chen's departure, would be remembered by its occupants, respectively, as two minutes of frustrated foot tapping, two minutes of mischievous giggling, and an uncertain quantity of minutes staring directly at the hands of the clock.

Freshly stapled results in hand, the geneticist's return marked an end to their silent chaos.

"Would you like to read the results yourself, professor Bonman, or would you prefer I explain them?"

"That will do just fine. What do we know?"

"We know that your concerns appear to be justified. The patient's calcium density, as you expected, has decreased. The inverse is true in hormones associated with the expression of uterine genes, where the results indicate a meteoric increase relative to the sample extracted on May 3rd - an approximate difference of six weeks. More immediate causes for concern, meanwhile, fall perfectly in line with those articulated in your notes. Namely," he adjusted a pair of reading glasses, more habit than necessity, "evidence of a significant depletion of glucose and electrolyte levels."

"How serious a depletion are we talking, Dr. Chen?"

"I would say that the results are nothing short of a cause for genuine alarm. It's as though the nutrients are being siphoned from her body more quickly than she can replenish them. I am… generally one to err on the side of trust, gentlemen, but I feel I would be remiss at this time not to echo a form of Ms. O'Lear's earlier sentiment."

Dr. Chen carried his eyes just above the page, scanning the room like a muffled boardslide clear across a skatepark rail.

"Why query the patient's DNA for a protogenesis gene? Why now, and, forgive me for asking, on what authority?"

Brady's intentions were to deflect, clear as carbon monoxide by the telltale squeeze of mental consternation on his face. Alvin didn't much see the point, and so reaffirmed in moments that fundamental tenet of sociality; whatever their aesthetic differences, the truth comes out more easily than the lie.

"Ma'am - that's her name, the patient - she's pregnant. Carrying an egg, rather. I'm not really sure if that's the same thing. And - just one egg. She was clear about that."

Guo's face turned to stone. Bitterness pinched Brady's lips into an impassable boundary. Even Melissa's snickering seemed to have been smothered by the wet cement of circumstance. Graced with an intermission of silence, a thing present in nauseating abundance during his time in a cell and confoundingly otherwise since, Alvin carried on.

"In any case, she's your patient, my student, Brady's objective, and all our responsibility. So I need you to lower the similarity threshold, Ms. O'Lear. A dozen times if you have to. All we need is the closest thing. We've been told there could be a transcription error -"

The woman before the computer and behind the suddenly implicated transcription software scoffed. For Alvin's part, he'd neglected his own sense of pride with too consistent an abandon to waste a neuron's weight in sodium on Melissa's self esteem.

"*We've been told there could be a transcription error.* Or an *inscription* error. Or any number of any shitload of things. Bare bones - we need to find the protogenesis gene, in whichever form, and establish whether or not it's causing the problems demonstrated by the results. Okay?"

"Of course."

"*I suppose.*"

"Thank you, Dr. Chen. And thank you, Ms. O'Lear. Brady - will you run back to the lab and make sure they get to work on addressing the shortage of electrolytes and - what was it?"

"Glucose."

"And the glucose. Doesn't have to be complicated. Supplements, capsules, a smoothie - whatever we need to get her leveled out while we sort out the gene problem. That's possible, right Guo? Stuffing her full of everything she's missing?"

"That is unclear, professor Bonman. As you may have inferred from my statement moments ago, the rate of diffusion seems to be independent of intake to a degree that the difference cannot be overcome by traditional means of supplementation. *Ma'am*, as per her patient records, is fed on demand. In other words - physiological uncertainties early in the project, in conjunction with standards regarding her ethical treatment, culminated in a policy of allowing the patient to dictate her own diet. Her meals and portions, in terms of glucose and electrolyte quantities ingested, have increased consistently throughout the last six weeks. And still we find that the densities of both are five percent short of sustainable."

"Five percent?"

"Just north of five percent, more precisely."

"I need *most* precisely, Guo."

Dr. Chen riffled through the results, wholly dependent on the cooperation of his glasses and pointer finger to converge on an answer.

"Five-point-two-two and five-point-one-eight percent, respectively."

"*Fuck me.*"

"Professor Bonman?"

The ruffles in his forehead concealed behind the palm of his hand, Alvin sidestepped the geneticist and shouldered through Brady to breathe down Melissa's neck, both victims of his urgency left to wallow in their confusion.

"Did you lower the threshold?"

"Sure did."

"And?"

"And…" she maintained Alvin's eyes for as long as it took to choreograph the keyboard command, an underhanded reminder of who between them was the expert, "… now we wait!"

"How long?"

"Ninety seconds. Less, more, hard to say. Should be long enough to apologize to lovely Mr. Chen, anyway. You've left the man unattended in the midst of a chat! A dreadful habit, that. I don't mean to scold, but poor Guo doesn't have it in him to speak up for himself."

"You have caused me no offense, professor Bonman." Alvin couldn't immediately tell whether that were true. "I do wish to understand your reaction, however, which I hope I can be forgiven for regarding as peculiar."

"Ask Brady."

"Me? What are you talking about?"

Brady's surprise was genuine. Alvin was glad for it - an opportunity to deliver his message more poignantly.

"I'm talking about the day you knocked on the door to my cell, Brady. I'm talking about the lecture you gave me on protocol - what not to do, what not to say, *when to leave*. I'm talking about the god damn reason we wake up at midnight once every three weeks to accommodate the sleep cycle of a herbivore from the fucking Permian."

"*Fuck me.*"

"If you're done fucking each other, gentlemen, I am pleased to say we have a match."

Like a herd of VCR era preteen boys jockeying for proximity to a screen where the only scene of Titanic they cared to watch drew nearer - Brady, Alvin, and even Guo moved with purpose for a glance at Melissa's success.

"*But* - I've had to mince the similarity threshold by forty percent to get it. So, effectively, this match tells us little about the patient's gene apart from enjoying a sequential overlap with the protogenesis sample *only just* sufficient to overcome the margin of error. It's impossible to say with certainty what the ultimate function of the matched gene is, or whether it's even been expressed in the patient at all."

"I wouldn't be so sure."

Alvin draped an arm across Guo's shoulders, drawing the geneticist in for a discussion artificially deprived of the slimmest room for misinterpretation.

"Twenty-two hours, forty-five minutes. One hour and fifteen minutes short of what your biological clock, and mine, and a dog, and a goldfish are wound to. That was the length of a day in the Permian. Better put - a five-point-two percent difference, *on the god damn nose*. Does that mean anything to you, Dr. Chen?"

"Nothing of consequence, professor Bonman. Patient records indicate no adverse health effects related to that incongruity between geological and biological time. Those are precisely the sorts of possibilities our laboratory technicians have made a point to remain vigilant of."

"That was the case as of Ma'am's last blood sample, six weeks back. We both know at least one thing that's changed since then. What *you* don't know is that she's begun to lactate - a *lot*. Almost as if her body believes the egg is already laid and ready to hatch, and the uterine hormones are so concentrated because they've only just hit their peak. Sounds to me like little Ma'am Jr. has a 21st century appetite on a Permian budget."

"If you are implying that the embryo - better described as a clone, mind you, given the presumed mechanism for its conception - diverged genetically from the mother such that it has begun to develop in accordance with a twenty-four hour day..."

Cheeks changing shade like an octopus to coral, the geneticist took a sharp breath he knew he would have been better served by rationing.

"Well, professor Bonman, I can only assert my authority on the subject and reject your prediction as mathematically false. The sheer *quantity* of genes involved in the formation and regulation of the pineal gland, or any primordial equivalent, for that matter, *forbids absolutely* any pretense of attribution to random genetic error. *Specifically* in the case of asexual reproduction. *Overwhelmingly* when further accounting for the incredible preponderance of less convenient genetic manifestations - each iteration of circadian alteration to be regarded as presenting an equal likelihood of incidence to yours. In layman's terms, *professor* Bonman, why twenty-four hours? Why not a twenty-five hour circadian rhythm? Why not a three hour day? Or a three day day! Simply said, you have a better chance of spontaneously combusting on your first day as president of Proxima Centauri b than you have of baring witness to such a coincidence. Nothing short of deliberate tinkering would bridge the difference *remotely*!"

Dr. Chen's glasses were askew, his face flush with passion dammed away for decades behind steel cliffs of political tact.

"There are no coincidences, Guo."

Alvin backed away, sorry he'd infringed upon the geneticists personal space but resolved he'd found what he needed there.

"Tell me, Dr. Chen. Is there such a thing? Deliberate tinkering?"

"Is there such a - *what? Such a thing as deliberate tinkering?*"

Guo's disposition seemed, as he tested, cleaned, and retested his glasses, not unlike a cyclist struggling to exchange insurance information with the driver who'd just concussed him.

"Does deliberate *genetic* tinkering exist? Is that your actual question, professor Bonman? Please do remind me which institution employs you. I would be delighted to visit the first public university built beneath a rock."

"Guo, you lovely man, I'm surprised at you!"

It was Melissa, of all people, to attempt a humanitarian outreach.

"I understand you've been under a great deal of stress, love, but that's no way to go about the business of answering questions asked in good faith. Even I wasn't privy to the specifics about your career until - what? A week in? Answer the man, Guo - it's not every day you get an open invitation to boast of your accolades for an audience eager to hear them."

Guo resembled a child on the playground, compelled by threat of administrative action to shake the hand of the boy with whom he'd traded insults from opposite ends of the monkey bars. Alvin, of course, felt no culpability in it - but he knew too much of people and their emotional idiosyncrasies to doubt whether Dr. Chen was having much the same thought.

"I'm sorry if my point was taken as an insult to your intelligence, Dr. Chen. That couldn't be further from the truth. If you'll just humor me, I think it's possible you'll come to share Melissa's perspective. This, all of this, has been in good faith."

"Humor you in which way, precisely?"

"Explain how, or whether, the sort of genetic tinkering you mentioned can be done."

"You genuinely aren't familiar with the CRISPR-Cas9 technique? Nor with the coming revolution in basic human experience to which it will have been absolutely formative?"

"Not exactly my area of expertise, Dr. Chen."

Guo seemed to cling to his doubt for another moment, unburdening himself of it at last and with the understanding that it was to be replaced by the bitter shame of presumptuousness.

"I am so very sorry for losing my temper, Alvin. I suppose a decade of authority over an intellectual echo chamber inhibits one's sense of the outside world and its hierarchies of attention."

"I've said worse things for similar reasons. Please Guo, just fill me in. We can decide how naive I am at the end. I promise."

"Very well. To be brief, developments in the study of 'Clustered Regularly Inter-spaced Short Palindromic Repeats', or sequences present in various microbial genomes unique for their repeating constituent patterns, encouraged my country's ruling party to establish a research laboratory dedicated entirely to investigating potential applications. As head of that team since its inception, I have also overseen independent recreations of various experiments with results considered fundamental to our efforts. One such endeavor involved reaffirming the function of *Cas9*, an enzyme so named for having been dynamically encoded by 'CRISPR Associated' families of genes. The great potential of CRISPR-Cas9 lay in that association, you see."

Alvin didn't yet see, but he had the academic acumen to imagine the direction and scope of Dr. Chen's CliffNotes memoir. Even Brady, self-admitted layman ever since his GPA's narrow escape from prerequisite STEM classes, was at minimum attentive and arguably intrigued.

"Between every twenty-nine pair repeating CRISPR sequence is one *non-repeating* thirty-two pair sequence called a 'spacer'; a name which forgivably minimized their importance while research was in its infancy. We now know that their function cannot be understated. Those sequences, though not repeating, are the very antithesis of *random*. In fact, they might most accurately be regarded as biological bits of memory. Studies since the early part of this century demonstrated that the spacers identified in various microbial specimens were *records* of external DNA, copied from the genome of threatening organisms or viruses with which they interacted, available thereafter to be referenced in the construction of enzymes purpose built to locate and disassemble identical invasive DNA. These microbes, effectively, evolved a universal vaccine at the molecular level - a biological mechanism to cut-and-paste genomic sequences so broad in its utility that a failure to exploit it medically would seem tantamount to genocide."

Guo plucked a handkerchief from his pants pocket by the frill, dabbing his eyes beneath the glasses.

"For our purposes, however, the key word to be considered is "microbial". No such function exists anywhere known in macro-biology, nor have we ourselves developed a procedural competence sufficient to influence the hormonal expression of an animal as it relates to circadian rhythm. I must reassert, with apology now and with humility, that your conclusion regarding the patient's imbalances *cannot* be attributed to any such distinction in her offspring's genome as it relates to her own. Statistics insist beyond doubt that so precise a divergence could not have occurred incidentally. Myself and all of science would agree that no mechanism, be it evolved naturally or incorporated artificially by a member of this team, exists which would have permitted whatsoever *deliberate tinkering* in any form."

"My dearest Dr. Chen?"

"Please, Ms. O'Lear, I would prefer Alvin be given the opportunity to respond while my explanation is most present on his mind."

"I don't think that will be necessary, love."

Flamingoes on two feet, the heads of all three men swung again toward Melissa's screen.

"This here-" Melissa implicated a specific portion of the Google search results with her pointer finger, "is that your beloved twenty-nine pair CRISPR gene, Guo?"

"Yes."

She cycled through the tabs, reminding herself not for the first time that afternoon to place more emphasis on organization. Eventually she arrived at a second page of responses.

"And this one - this appears to be an adequate pre-ellipses, comma delimited representation of the list of ninety-three aforementioned Cas genes, is it not?"

"Yes. I am pleased you've taken an interest in learning, Ms. O'Lear, but if you wouldn't mind…"

Melissa snatched him by the cold shoulder.

"One more thing, love, and then I promise you're free to go."

A click of the mouse and her software's interface returned to the forefront of the screen. Another, and a PDF of her latest query's results were generated.

"Those there, heading either column of results returned from the query I ran as you, for lack of a better term, *droned* on about your trade - do you see them? Each is one of the two conditions I defined as the parameters of the query. An *either* this *or* that sort of scenario. That said - would you agree that either sequence following the words '*Sequence is Identical to…*' is an accurate representation of the repeating bits of CRISPR and all the lovely Cas genes, respectively?"

"They are, Ms. O'Lear."

"And would you be so kind as to announce the results listed thereafter for the less familiar in attendance?"

Guo tested, cleaned, and retested his glasses, attempted to do read aloud as had been asked of him, and vomited instead.

Melissa, for her part, remained polite throughout the near miss. For the first time in Alvin's presence she vacated her seat, rolling her chair aside by hand in place of foot to create an avenue to her computer that didn't intersect the puddle of breakfast and Jade oolong tea.

"Pinch your nose and have a look, professor."

Brady wasn't certain whether it were from the smell or the anticipation, but he came dangerously close to a spill of his own more than once during the thirty seconds Alvin spent reading and rejecting and rereading the document.

"Al, times up. Just read the damn thing and give me the short version."

"There are matches to Ma'am's DNA for both conditions."

"So what's that mean for us, precisely?"

"It means that genetic tinkering isn't off the table."

Part sense of urgency, part wounded pride in a room swollen with genius worthy of international esteem, Brady tried his best to ask meaningful questions.

"But - who is tinkering? Ma'am hatched, grew, spoke, predicted some accurate shit, predicted some outlandish shit, and… and she is what she is! Why would her *chick* be any different when its DNA has every reason to be identical to hers? Crispy genes or no crispy genes?"

Melissa secretly enjoyed the feeling of delivering news of a vomit inducing quality, and saw in Brady her next opportunity.

"It's a good question, but you've already answered it yourself in a way, Mr. Thomas. Ma'am hatched, but not from an egg laid by a mother. She was assembled, *by us*, from a medley of basic elements combined and animated as per the precise instructions of *that genome* carved into *those rocks*. Her offspring, should it survive long enough to do justice to that title, will rise from the same medley - but with different instructions."

"And why is that?"

As a mother would do for her child had she found him retching from a knee, Melissa absently stroked Dr. Chen's back.

"For the same reason we couldn't find the protogenesis gene without lowering the threshold, lovely Brady. The CRISPR and Cas family matches, every last one of them, fall *within* the boundaries of the Komodo Dragon gene derivative. It says so right here in the results.

"Ours is a conundrum of genotype versus phenotype; genetic existence versus genetic expression. It is a complicated distinction that I, now approaching a year spent at what amounts to Space Camp for geneticists, have learned to frame in terms of an analogy and adjust when appropriate. Imagine, if you will, the protogenesis gene to be a small town, and afterward that the gene can be regarded as *expressed* if and only if that town constructs a new school. Everybody in town knows everybody, nobody sells their houses - feel free to include as many cliches as you like.

"A *dreadful* fire, representing - for the purposes of our analogy - organic asexual impregnation, devastates the next town over. Chief among the consequences is the hurried relocation of its substantially different population to our own charming little neighborhood. Among the newcomers are CRISPR families, friendly enough, and Cas gene families, too. The CRISPR parents bring their darling little thirty-two pair spacers along, and the Cas couples, envious, set to work producing enzymes to fill their new homes with laughter. With so many knowledge-starved younglings running about, and so abruptly amenable the tax base, our town commissions a new school be built."

Melissa grinned from cheek to cheek, still stoking Guo's back as though he were not a decade and a half her senior.

"That *will* be the case for Ma'am's little one, anyway. As for Ma'am herself, any instructions for splicing bits of existing genes were never expressed because *protogenesis was not the mechanism* for her conception nor her resultant gestational development. She's not a miracle virgin birth, she's a test tube baby. We doused the fire ourselves before it had the chance to build the school."

"But - but how different can they possibly be? Different sleep cycles, eye colors? How many edits are we talking about here and what does that mean exactly?"

When at last Dr. Chen had gotten his stomach under control and his legs underneath him, he drew the handkerchief across his lips, laid it flat atop the pool of bile, and managed to thank Melissa for her comfort without imposing his breath upon her.

"Over one-hundred-thousand CRISPR matches, about half as many Cas genes detected. Fifty-thousand edits to her genome. At the very least, Mr. Thomas, it means an individual no more identical to Ma'am than I from my brother or you from your son. It means tinkering, and of the most deliberate sort."

Alvin was reminded, by the degree of their departure from one absurdity to another, of which between them necessitated his involvement in the first place.

"What does it mean for Ma'am?"

"If the results are to be believed -"

Guo straightened his collar on the way to the door, himself undecided as to whether his next destination would be the lab or the sick bay.

"- then the egg must be removed without delay. So, professor Bonman, I suppose it means we should make her comfortable."

INSTALLMENT SEVEN

"Welcome back. In response to the authority's case articulated this morning regarding charges of 'Wanton Obstruction of Protocols Two, Five, and One', ordered here by magnitude of severity, Dr. Bo Nilsson has expressed intentions to speak in his own defense. In so doing, and in full awareness of the fact, he forfeits any claim to rights of abstention should the panel be inclined to request any clarification, elaboration, or whichsoever detail it deems pertinent. Dr. Nilsson, you are invited to take the stand."

"An invitation graciously accepted, and an introduction warmly regarded. Thank you."

Bo nestled into the makeshift stand, lowly beside the makeshift judge on his makeshift bench. Of that conference space - arranged into a courtroom as if by memory and staffed as if by Joseph Stalin - Bo Nilsson, wherever it was he sat or stood, was focal. Now he smiled at the man selected to preside over the occasion, one judge of a panel of seven, his vote equal in weight and his authority restricted only by the altitude of his fancies. The retirement-averse Texan was haggard and stooped and jowled by chronic discontent, and Bo would not have smiled but for the mental image of this man in a Victorian wig.

"Feel free, Dr. Nilsson."

"A potent choice of words, your honor, and an opportune foundation from which to support my initial postulation; the outcome of this tribunal should be my immediate release in light of time served.

"Tragically, it has been some four months since I've had cause to *feel free*, as you say. Four months counting stitches on a padded wall for entertainment. Four months pacing from bed to bath for exercise. Four months conducting my hygienic affairs in a space so lacking in privacy that the Ancient Greeks would consider it an affront to basic sexual modesty.

"Allow me to put it another way. If floors and ceilings are to be excluded, a position I myself have come to endorse, the simple arithmetic of my incarceration yields just *one* padded wall's worth of intellectual stimulation per *thirty-day* experiment in the most reprehensible incivility. If one were to remove their perspective altogether from the inhumane square-footage contained therein, one might question with some measure of distaste why my arithmetic is such when all the world outside those walls seems all the more positive for my actions."

"More positive how, Dr. Nilsson?"

"Why, in every imaginable way - if that constitutes a legal answer. If the whispers passed between my chaperones are of any citable merit, the very action for which I am condemned is part and parcel of the innumerable successes of this project during the period of my detention."

The presiding authority glowered his displeasure with the men entrusted with Bo's supervision, stood now on either side of the doctor even on the stand. To be informed in broad daylight that his discretion protocols were so grossly neglected was a poor start to the proceedings.

"And which successes are those?"

"To be fair, only the two discussed at most length by these fellows are known to me in any detail. Of the rest, I could only venture to assume a… general preponderance of human progress by the degree of inarticulate jubilation to be heard from the far side of my cell door. Fortunately for myself, and for transparency in law no matter the jurisdiction, those successes seem to be of incontrovertible value."

"Get to the point Dr. Nilsson."

"Very well. Success one: the preservation of the project to which we all can attribute our livelihoods, in one form or another. Were it not for my quick thinking in a moment that demanded nothing less, I could not have been expected to reach a definitive conclusion regarding the patient's condition. Critically, Alvin Bonman would have been given no reason to suspect pregnancy, context sensitive investigation of the patient's blood would not have taken place with sufficient urgency, the patient would have perished in two days time under the *best* of circumstances, and the egg she nurtured will only have been discovered half rotten on a single-use, aluminum foil autopsy table."

"You are some thespian, Bo."

The presiding juror shuffled through a stack of documents prepared for him pre-hearing. A gavel there kept the papers in place, that icon of judicial power designated only secondarily for use as a prop should he choose to embark upon his own displays of legal theater.

"What you've failed to mention in your statement - or in any statement since the twelfth day of your detainment, a point which we can presume to coincide with your learning of the patient's death and the survival of her offspring - is the original sentiment you expressed to this panel. Do you recall that sentiment?"

"The law is not sentimental, your honor."

"Being cute will get you nowhere, Dr. Nilsson."

"Might I ask whether you are speaking from experience, sir?"

Red cheeked, the judge waited until those in the room with protective vests of seniority stopped giggling.

"Answer the question or *nobody* will be speaking in your defense."

"Very well, your honor. My original intention was to persuade the authority that Ma'am-"

"Please identify *Ma'am* for the record."

"- was to persuade the authority that Ma'am, my proto-mammalian patient of several months, had exposed herself as a threat to our species by actively withholding from us her capacity to asexually reproduce. That said, please consider the following with all possible attention. Though I have and do willingly retract, as a matter of court record and in light of developments since my incarceration, my very temporary belief in the efficacy of any preemptive mitigation of those threats, the legal distinction between *intent* and *action* deserves to be made and with unrepentant emphasis.

"Whereas my *intent*, as you've described it, was to acquire critical information regarding the patient and so provide the authority with an informed recommendation, my *actions* were no more criminal than a stark poke to the sternum of a passing stranger. Perhaps that stranger might take some offense to my action, unconvinced I'd behaved prudently in pursuit of her attention. But if I were to point out the telltale hue of jaundice in her eyes, recommend an emergency room and a dialysis clinic, and her life were spared by the coincidence of our intersecting - why, I can only assert that any damages incurred in the course of poking would be laughed out of court, and the complainant, pursuant to the absolute minimum standard of rational discourse, ridiculed for photographing the bruise."

"Dully noted. We've all had quite enough of your antics, Dr. Nilsson. Please proceed with all possible brevity to your second 'success'."

"Your honor - *my pleasure.*"

Bo used his hand as a blinder so only the audience would know he winked.

"As a direct result of my actions, the patient's egg survived surgical extraction, hatching, and infancy. To reiterate - none of the above could have come to pass were it not for the exposure to risk I assumed; my health and freedom placed in jeopardy so that the authority's ignorance of Ma'am's pregnancy might be dispelled.

"Today, meanwhile, the adolescent shows no signs of the sensory inhibition experienced by its mother in the months before her death. Consequently, the adolescent's unimpeded access to so-called quantum nuance provided the authority, via multiple consultants retained after Ma'am's death, with the exact date of an minor eruption of the Yellowstone Caldera. Forewarning permitted the evacuation of human populations and livestock within an area encompassing portions of Wyoming, Idaho, and Montana. Minor though the eruption was, no loss of life constitutes a *success*, say I, if ever there was one."

The judge was seething, and Bo's pair of gossip-prone armed guards had no seats to slouch in. The defendant between them coughed politely, a smile threatening the corner of his lips.

"Your honor?"

"*What?*"

"Have I the right to call a witness to the stand?"

"You do, although whether that call is answered depends entirely on the whims of the witness."

Bo canvassed the modest crowd, a single grey hair come at last to divide his face in two.

"What say you, professor Bonman? I've scratched your back, haven't I?"

"Are you going to have me take an oath or anything?"

"Only if you plan on lying, Mr. Bonman."

131

"I'm good. Ready when he is, your honor."

Alvin looked very much uncomfortable on the witness stand, all things considered. Compounded no doubt by his earlier appearance before this same ramshackle courtroom, twice seeing his net-worth halved by real judges stateside hadn't left a taste in his mouth he considered deserving of third course. Bo, strangely, had the appearance of being sympathetic to *his* plight.

"Don't be nervous, Alvin. We're all friends here."

"I'm not nervous, Dr. Nilsson. Can't say whether I've decided we're friends, either."

"I am very sorry to have assumed. Might I ask, though, whether you consider my advising you on my suspicions of Ma'am's pregnancy as a *friendly* thing to do? I am referring, of course, to our brief meeting on the day of my alleged misconduct,"

"I guess you could say that. It certainly wasn't *unfriendly*. Depends on whether you classify friendliness as existing on a spectrum."

"Do you?"

"Sure."

"And would you be willing to ascribe the same basic format to a metric such as - trust, let's say? Would it be sensible to imagine such a spectrum where *one* implies indisputable untrustworthiness, and where *ten* can be taken to mean absolute trustworthiness?"

"That seems reasonable. Are you going to ask me where I think you fit on that spectrum, Bo?"

"I was not planning on it, Alvin. I'd sooner ask where, in your view, Ma'am herself might best be placed. And it seems only right to mention in advance of your answer that adherence to the adage of *speak not ill of the dead* is no legal requirement. I've looked."

The audience of four dozen faculty and six panel members reservedly laughed, and Alvin felt more at ease, if only just.

"She was not particularly trustworthy, in my experience. Willing to do whatever she needed to do to get whatever it was she needed to get. There were some redeeming qualities, I guess. Enough to give her a *three* and feel like I'm not rounding up."

"Three? That doesn't sound very trustworthy to me, professor Bonman. Why so low?"

Alvin tried to isolate the best of a whole litany of answers, all readily available and clearly defined in his mind and still somehow impossible to count.

"She pretended to struggle with geology to get into a room with me, although I won't say I hold that one against her. She funneled my thoughts into a mental spreadsheet as they popped into my head and lied about how she knew what I'd say before I said it. Worst, probably, was when-"

Alvin retraced his steps toward an empty seat near the back of the room. Brady occupied the next chair over and was, by all appearances, no more cheerful about the exchange than his friend who was a party to it. It was a game of double dutch; Alvin and Bo each holding their end of that line of questioning, Brady first in line to skip.

"The worst, I think, was when she convinced me that the authority would kill me if the project were to end unexpectedly. It wasn't five minutes later that she implied, strongly, that Brady's children had a fatal mitochondrial disease that he wouldn't be privy to without lending his assistance."

Murmuring, chatter; in all, two parts sympathy, one part shock, two parts exasperation.

"So you would say you were coerced? Is that accurate, Alvin?"

"About as accurate as it gets."

"And - would it be absurd to imagine that coercion was a means Ma'am was liable to carry on practicing for whichsoever end she fancied?"

"That's enough, Dr. Nilsson. Find a direction that doesn't blatantly conflict with your earlier retraction, or find your seat."

"Fair enough, your honor."

Bo's fingers were woven behind his back, his eyes pleasant and predatory.

"Alvin - professor Bonman, though it's true you give the impression of a man not altogether comfortable in the lurid spotlight of this courtroom, I wouldn't go so far as to describe you as a person afraid for his life. Have I taken too many liberties in saying that?"

"Not at all. I'm not in love with this room, or this seat, but I don't look over my shoulder when I'm walking down the hallway."

"And why not?"

"*Why not?*"

"Why not fear for your life? You've only just said that Ma'am levied some lofty accusations against the authority, a threat to your existence chief among them. What changed, professor Bonman?"

An authority among the authority, the judge's fingers twitched for the gavel. His restraint was well founded and better received by the other six members of the panel, each doubtless aware of the mental strife Bo's tactics would elicit. Forbidding the defendant from continuing to pursue this sensitive, albeit incontestably relevant, issue would seem tantamount to an admission of the authority's guilt. Allowing it was slightly more tolerable - at worst, Bo Nilsson's case would be proven, his good name restored, and his sentence commuted. Later, when the attention had waned and his paranoia rationalized, Bo's predetermined fate could be secured less publicly.

"Well, everything. Everything has changed."

"Would you mind boiling that response down for the court, Alvin?"

"I can certainly try."

Alvin did try, certainly, and in a few moments had formulated a response respectful to the oath he hadn't been asked to give.

"Our efforts in the days before Ma'am's death-"

"Briefly, whose efforts? For the record."

"Sorry, I am referring to Brady Thomas and myself."

"Very well, carry on."

"Our efforts in the days before Ma'am's death allowed for various conclusions to be drawn regarding the irreversible decline of her own health and, conversely, the immediate viability of her egg. In that vein, our involvement led directly to the discovery of an overlooked protogenesis gene and the existence of chromosomal modification sequences encoded into it. Even Ma'am didn't give us any reason to think she was aware of their existence. Point being - the egg survived extraction, and any notions of *discontinuing the project* were tabled in light of the gradual realization that those sequences, with the exception of modernizing her Circadian rhythm, were designed to modify traits believed to differentiate between individuals of the species, rather than to synthesize some ten foot venom spewing monster. Not to put ourselves on a pedestal, but what we did saved this project, saved Ma'am's comparably pleasant offspring, and saved a few thousand North Western farmers and their herds. *So far.*

"As for why I don't spend every day of my life bedridden by existential worry… The authority, and I say this with all possible respect and then some, would be insane to bite the hand that fed them."

Smugness born in Bo's eyes were channelled through a network of wrinkles until no part of his face was unexplored.

"That is a conviction we share. It seems we share quite a lot, you and I, professor Bonman, not least of all a history of concerted effort toward maintaining the efficacy of this project. Truth be told, if looked upon through a lense impeccable of bias, one could have reason to believe that your answer now, and my testimony before, present much the same argument. Your actions, and Mr. Thomas's actions, were catalyzed by my own - and so it can be said that any retribution owed to you on the part of the authority as established by the series of events that ensued would, and should, and are not, *equally* or *doubly* due to the man who set them in motion, can it not? Where we overlap most apparently, professor Bonman, is in an endeavor of righteousness. Where we diverge most principally, or so says the evidence, is in equity of reward."

The response transcended chatter, and the judge took his paperweight by the handle and thrice struck the desk.

"*Enough!*"

His jowls swayed from the impact and the passion.

"This courtroom will *not* be governed by emotion. Nor will your theatrics be allowed to poison this project for another moment, Dr. Nilsson. It is clear to everyone in attendance that your questions are leading by design and their aim to elicit a springboard for your rhetoric. Repeat that behavior and you will be returned to your cell so I might spare the people in this room the intellectual decay to be expected by your proximity. Have I made myself clear?"

"Yes, your honor."

"Good. You have five minutes, and they began two minutes ago."

"Then I will get to it. Professor Bonman, have you any other credible assurances of your wellbeing? Anything ongoing, or forthcoming, perhaps, which guarantees your continuing utility to the authority beyond a debt of gratitude they'd just as soon be inclined to forget?"

"What could that possibly have to do with you, Bo? Say we have a lot in common all you want, that doesn't make me a signatory."

"Suffice it to say, mine are not the only intentions on trial this morning. *Quo Bono* goes the phrase, I think. Please answer the question now, Alvin, lest I allow you to develop a springboard complex."

"Alright, yes. I'm conferring with Ma'am's offspring. I was requested by name the day she was fitted with a modulator. Refused to speak with anyone else until I was added to the list."

That affirmation was all Bo considered necessary toward illuminating the authority's hypocrisy in punishment as symptomatic of their dystopian placement of utility over equity. Any remaining time was his to spend on stimulating his mind and sating a desire for social interaction so long and so comprehensively deprived to him.

"*Conferring*? Not consulting? Has the nomenclature changed?"

"There isn't a thing I can teach her about geology that she doesn't already know."

"If not geology, then to what do these conferences pertain?"

"The short version?"

No one in attendance was naive enough to believe that Alvin's question was Bo's to answer. The judge glanced at his watch and growled, "two minutes."

"Some sort of 'symbiosis' between our species. She's more idealistic than Ma'am, no question about that. Less Jedi mind trick, more *Kumbaya*."

"That's lovely. You also discuss potential hazards to mankind, isn't that true? Given that we already know of one tragedy she's helped us to forego."

"Kind of. She's very careful about how she goes about answering those types of questions. It's caused some frustration, to put it lightly."

"I can only imagine. Has she explained the reason for her reluctance to you, Alvin? It seems counter to her character, at least as you've presented it, to hesitate while people's lives teeter in the balance. People she describes as worthy of a place in her symbiosis, no less."

"She did."

"And?"

"And it's complicated."

"Ninety-seconds, Dr. Nilsson."

"Noted, your honor. Ninety-seconds, Alvin. Please try your best to whittle her explanation to its most concise."

"She, *fuck*... She has to avoid directly precalling - observing in advance - any human activity when at all possible. If she precalls a sentient action, as she put it, and then attempts to dissuade, redirect, or otherwise influence the person who took it, the curtains fall and the whole thing goes to shit.

"Let's say - let's say that instead of measuring the amount of pressure beneath the Yellowstone Caldera, she'd just precalled a farmer in Idaho getting buried alive in soot. The moment she tried to send him a cryptic warning in the mail, that would be it. Her wires would fray at the edges and she'd go blind to quantum nuance. Maybe the farmer and his kids and his cows escape, great, but she never saw the tornado brewing above the next town over. Anything she hadn't already observed would be inaccessible; lost behind a boundary. When we asked whether the effects were permanent, she said she'd formed a hypothesis - her words - that the longevity of that boundary corresponds directly to the number of people influenced after precollection. That struck everyone as odd."

"Why is that?"

"Nobody was really sure when she found the time. She wasn't even two months hatched."

"And you believe her explanation, do you?"

"I didn't at first."

"Until?"

"Until I asked her about the solar flare her mother had predicted. She laughed. Stuck out like a severed thumb because it was the first time I'd heard either of them do that."

"Laughed why?"

"Hard to say. But I don't think I could forget what she followed up with if you hypnotized me."

"What was that, professor Bonman?"

"*Never will the world have seen a lie told to its greater benefit. If only she'd minded the harsh lessons with half the attention she paid the convenient ones.*"

Bo was taken aback for the first time he could recall. Even the sight of Ma'am's sail unfurling before him, even the taste of the milk on his tongue; even those had not struck him with such force that the gears in his minds were ground to a halt. The doctor was taken aback, and he would regret the tax he paid in seconds.

"What does that have to do with her blindness to - to *quantum nuance*? How-"

"Time is up, Dr. Nilsson."

"Please, your honor, one more question."

"*Your time is up, Dr. Nilsson.* Gentlemen, see him to his cell and be damn sure there isn't a word between you. The last thing I want to do tomorrow is reconvene this court with a new pair of co-defendants."

"Your honor, I beg you!"

"Good bye, Bo. We'll be sure to let you know how deliberations went."

Dr. Nilsson's appeals were many, heard in echoes long after his stone faced detail whisked him from sight. Most of the audience was already making for the same door when the stenographer whispered a concern into the judge's ear.

"Stay put, people. Just a little clerical matter to clear up and then you'll get your bathroom breaks. Professor Bonman, would you be so kind as to state the name of Ma'am's 'offspring'? I'm told it didn't come up, but we'll need it if we mean to keep our records tidy."

"I would love to, your honor, but she hasn't decided on one."

"Decided? Was she given a book of baby names and a deadline?"

"Not exactly. We asked her what she'd like to be referred to and she rattled off two possibilities, on the spot. Since then, any time I ask her to pick between them she just... freezes up."

"Well, far be it from us to judge her for it. But we do need to jot something down. I'll tell you what. Give me the options, we'll choose our favorite, and maybe she'll feel inclined to agree."

"Can't argue with that. Fair warning - they're unconventional."

"I'm sure I've seen worse. The first name?"

"The letter 'P', a dash, *zero-zero-one*."

"And the second?"

"*P-999*. Same format."

"Well, doesn't that have a nice ring to it?"

ABOUT THE AUTHOR

Devyn's unique approach to science fiction as a genre has inspired
tens of people, although there is speculation that that figure may now
be in the dozens. He attended Florida State University, graduating
pseudo cum laude with a major in Political Science and a Minor-In-
Possession.

Made in the USA
Monee, IL
16 January 2022

89127858R00083